"*Rabbit Hole* is a sensitive drama with the well-observed poignancy of a memorable short story, captured with the blinkered belief of Lindsay-Abaire's grief-stricken heart."

—Charles McNulty, *Los Angeles Times*

"GRADE: A! A transcendent and deeply affecting new play, which shifts perfectly from hilarity to grief."

—Whitney Pastorek, *Entertainment Weekly*

"*Rabbit Hole* presents a tragedy and its consequences with utter candor, and without sentimentality. The dialogue is most impressive for capturing the awkwardness and pain of thinking people faced with an unthinkable situation—and eventually, their capacity for survival, and even hope."

—Elyssa Gardner, *USA Today*

"With *Rabbit Hole*, David Lindsay-Abaire has crafted the most serious, simply told work of his career—a painstakingly beautiful, dramatically resourceful, exquisitely human new play."

—Leonard Jacobs, *Backstage*

"A thoroughly absorbing, profoundly affecting and painfully touching examination of grief."

—Robert Feldberg, *Bergen Record*

"The highest praise to playwright David Lindsay-Abaire! *Rabbit Hole* is an entertaining and satisfying play—it might just be the year's best."

—Gena Hymowech, *Show Business Weekly*

"A perceptive and poignant study in the day-to-day aches of bereavement: problems with personal intimacy, the uneasy friends who don't call, the emptiness in a house packed with reminders . . . Heartbreaking in its theme and details, *Rabbit Hole* is a beautifully crafted work of great sensitivity."

—Michael Sommers, *Star-Ledger*

Rabbit Hole

Rabbit Hole

David Lindsay-Abaire

THEATRE COMMUNICATIONS GROUP
NEW YORK
2010

Rabbit Hole is published by Theatre Communications Group, Inc.,
520 Eighth Avenue, 24th Floor, New York, NY 10018-4156

This publication is made possible in part with public funds from the New York State Council on the Arts, a State Agency.

TCG books are exclusively distributed to the book trade by Consortium Book Sales and Distribution, 1045 Westgate Drive, St. Paul, MN 55114.

LIBRARY OF CONGRESS CATALOGING-IN-PUBLICATION DATA

Lindsay-Abaire, David.
Rabbit hole / by David Lindsay-Abaire. — 1st ed.
p. cm.
ISBN-13: 978-1-55936-0
1. Bereavement—Drama. 2. Spouses—Drama. I. Title.
PS3562.I511925R33 2006
812'.6—dc22
2006011673

Cover design by Chip Kidd
Cover photo by Mark Tucker
Book design and composition by Lisa Govan

First Edition, June 2006
New Edition, December 2010

Rabbit Hole

Production History

Rabbit Hole was commissioned by South Coast Repertory (Martin Benson, Artistic Director; David Emmes, Producing Artistic Director) in Costa Mesa, CA. It received its world premiere by Manhattan Theatre Club (Lynne Meadow, Artistic Director; Barry Grove, Executive Producer) on Broadway at the Biltmore Theatre, on February 2, 2006. The production was directed by Daniel Sullivan. The set design was by John Lee Beatty, the costume design was by Jennifer Von Mayrhauser, the lighting design was by Christopher Akerlind and the original music and sound design were by John Gromada. The production stage manager was Roy Harris. The cast included:

BECCA	Cynthia Nixon
IZZY	Mary Catherine Garrison
HOWIE	John Slattery
NAT	Tyne Daly
JASON	John Gallagher, Jr.

Characters

BECCA: late thirties/early forties

IZZY: early thirties, Becca's sister

HOWIE: late thirties/early forties, Becca's husband

NAT: mid-sixties, Becca and Izzy's mother

JASON: a seventeen-year-old boy

Place

Larchmont, New York

Time

The present

Act One

Scene One

Late February. A spacious eat-in kitchen.

Saturday afternoon. Becca, late thirties, is folding the laundry, kids clothes, and putting it in neat piles on the table. Her sister, Izzy, early thirties, is in the middle of a story, getting herself a glass of orange juice from the fridge.

IZZY

And then I see her across the bar, coming at me with this *look*, you know. And everybody kinda steps aside for her, like the Red Sea, or whatever—just clears a path for her, and I'm like, "What's with *this* nut-job?"

BECCA

But you don't even know this woman.

IZZY

Never seen her before. I was just sitting there with Reema. Do you remember Reema?

BECCA

No.

IZZY

She's a friend of mine. I was sitting there with Reema, and suddenly this lady is in my face. And she's all sweaty and yelling and *really* pissed.

BECCA

Why?

IZZY

I don't even *know* at this point. It has something to do with her boyfriend, who's apparently at the end of the bar.

BECCA

Were you flirting or—?

IZZY

No, I don't even know who she's *talking* about. So she's all up in my face, and her breath is like—

BECCA

Boozy?

IZZY

Yeah boozy, but even worse, you know, like there's something rancid stuck to the roof of her mouth.

BECCA

Ew.

IZZY

Rotting peanut butter or something.

BECCA

Good lord, Izzy.

IZZY

And she's harassing me, and blowing her stank-breath in my face. And cussing. My god, you wouldn't believe the words that came out of this lady's mouth.

BECCA

And you don't even know who she's talking about.

IZZY

She's talking about her boyfriend.

BECCA

No, I know but—

IZZY

Auggie.

(Beat.)

BECCA

Oh. I thought you didn't know who she—

IZZY

No, at the *time* I didn't know who she was talking about, because I didn't know he was *there*. But then I figured it out later, "Oh, she must be Auggie's girlfriend."

BECCA

So you know him.

IZZY

Yeah, I know him, but still. Lemme finish.

BECCA

I'm sorry.

IZZY

So she's all, "You bitch, you. Fuck you, you bitch."

BECCA

Izzy—

IZZY

Sorry: "F-U, you B," and all that. Just talking like a maniac.

BECCA

Uh-huh.

IZZY

And people are looking at us, so I'm starting to feel self-conscious.

BECCA

Of course.

IZZY

And she's just going off, and I can't really *do* anything because the place is so crowded, you know? And she's a big lady. Real hefty. More chins than—what does Mom say?

BECCA

More Chins than a Chinese phone book.

IZZY

Exactly. So I can't even get around her to escape or whatever. And I'm starting to feel *violated*, you know?

BECCA

Sure.

IZZY

My personal space, and my dignity, or what have you, so I just made a fist, hauled off, and BOOM!

(Beat.)

BECCA

What does that mean?

IZZY

It means I hit her.

BECCA

No, you didn't.

IZZY

Crazy, right?

BECCA

You hit her?

IZZY

Yeah. Right in the face. BOOM. She went down.

BECCA

Oh my god, Izzy. —You *hit* that woman?

IZZY

I couldn't get around her. And she was screaming like a retard.

BECCA

Izzy—

IZZY

What would *you* have done?

BECCA

Well I certainly wouldn't have hit her. Jesus.

IZZY

And you know what they don't tell ya? It really hurts. To punch someone. It frickin' hurts.

BECCA

Well, yeah.

IZZY

They don't put that on TV. It's all, "Now that oughtta show him." But for me it was like, "Mother*fucker*, that *killed*!" Look at my knuckles. *(Shows her; then off Becca's look)* What?

BECCA

Nothing.

IZZY

You don't approve?

BECCA

I didn't say that.

IZZY

This lady was *at* me.

BECCA

I know. I didn't say anything.

IZZY

But you wanna though.

(Beat.)

BECCA

I just worry about you.

IZZY

Don't worry about me. *She* was the one on the floor.

BECCA

That's not what I meant. You were in a bar fight.

IZZY

So?

BECCA

A *bar fight*, Izzy.

IZZY

She was up in my face!

BECCA

I know, but it's so . . .

IZZY

What?

BECCA

Jerry Springer.

IZZY

What's that supposed to mean? You think I'm trashy?

BECCA

You punched a woman in the face!

IZZY

She provoked me!

BECCA

Were you drunk?

IZZY

No.

BECCA

I thought you were getting it together.

IZZY

Don't judge me.

BECCA

You said you were gonna take it easy.

IZZY

Man, Becca. Why do you have to—?

BECCA

You can't be doing this kinda stuff, Izzy. You're not a kid anymore.

IZZY

I didn't realize there was a cut-off date.

BECCA

Well there should be. For acting like a jackass there *should* be a cut-off date. Were you on anything?

IZZY

Oh my god.

BECCA

Were you?

IZZY

No. Man, why did I say anything to you?

BECCA

I don't know. Why *did* you?

IZZY

Look, I went out. I got into a fight. I thought it was a funny story. I thought you'd be amused.

BECCA

I'm not.

IZZY

Clearly.

BECCA

I thought you were gonna go easy, that's all. That you were gonna do less of this.

IZZY

Hey, I'm still coping, too, Becca. I know it's not the same, but it's still hard. Okay?

(Beat.)

BECCA

Don't do that.

IZZY

Do what?

BECCA

Gimme a break.

IZZY

What? I'm not allowed to be *upset* anymore?

BECCA

No, you're not allowed to *use* him.

IZZY

What are you—?

BECCA

As an excuse.

IZZY

I'm *not.*

BECCA

You're not allowed to use him to justify your own shit. Just don't do that. Please.

(Silence. Becca folds the clothes.)

IZZY

That's not what I was doing.

BECCA

Okay.

IZZY

I'm hungry. Mind if I get something?

BECCA

Since when do you ask?

IZZY

You're making me feel sensitive.

(Izzy heads back to the fridge.)

Where's Howie?

BECCA

He's with Rick. They're playing squash.

IZZY

(Chuckles) Squash.

(Regarding something in the fridge) What's this? Pudding?

BECCA

It's gonna be crème caramel.

IZZY

Howie's a lucky man. Ya won't see *me* making anyone crème caramel.

BECCA

If you're hungry, Isabel, grab something. Don't stand there with the door open.

IZZY

(Holds up an individual crème caramel) Can I have one of these? There's an extra in here.

(Beat.)

BECCA

Yeah, okay.

IZZY

Well I won't eat it if you don't want me to.

BECCA

No, go ahead. You're right, there's an extra.

IZZY

You sure?

BECCA

Just let me finish it.

IZZY

I can eat it like this.

BECCA

No. Then it's just custard.

IZZY

I like custard.

BECCA

I didn't make custard, I made crème caramel.

(Becca gets a dessert plate, and over the following she takes the ramekin and runs a knife around the inside edge of it.)

How's work?

IZZY

Don't ask me that please.

BECCA

Why not?

(Beat.)

You got fired?

IZZY

It never ends with me, does it.

BECCA

Not often, no.

IZZY

Don't tell Mom.

BECCA

How can you get fired from Applebee's?

IZZY

It was all politics. I don't really wanna get into it.

(Becca flips the ramekin over onto the plate, and the crème caramel comes out. She gets a spoon and hands both to Izzy.)

Thank you.

(Becca wipes down the counter, cleans up. Izzy pokes at the caramel with her spoon.)

I like how it oozes.

BECCA

Of course you do.

IZZY

(Takes a bite) Mmmmm.

BECCA

Better than custard, isn't it?

IZZY

Yes it is. You were right. Again.

(Beat.)

And again and again and again.

(Becca goes back to folding clothes.)

I wasn't using him as an excuse. I was just saying that it's been hard to pull it together, that's all. For all of us.

BECCA

Izzy, please.

IZZY

And I *wasn't* drinking when I hit that lady. Stone sober.

BECCA

Yeah *right*.

IZZY

I *was*. I just had soda that night.

(We hear the dryer buzz.)

BECCA

She gonna press charges, ya think?

IZZY

No, Auggie would kill her. She's over it anyway. She moved out. Went to her cousin's or something.

(Becca, on her way to the laundry room, stops.)

BECCA

What are you talking about?

IZZY

She moved. Out of Auggie's place. They're not together anymore.

BECCA

(Confused; comes back) I'm sorry . . . Do you *know* these people?

IZZY

Auggie I do. The girlfriend I only *heard* about.

(Beat.)

BECCA

What'd you do, Izzy?

IZZY

Whadaya mean?

BECCA

To that woman. What'd you *do* to her?

IZZY

I told you, I hit her.

BECCA

Before that.

IZZY

Nothing. That was the first time I met her.

BECCA

People don't scream in your face for no reason.

IZZY

Sure they do. You should get out more.

BECCA

Were you sleeping with him? This Auggie guy, whatever his name is? You were sleeping with him, right?

(Beat.)

IZZY

Where ya goin' with this?

BECCA

Well Jesus, Iz, you tell this story like you're an innocent bystander. You say you don't know *who* this woman was—

IZZY

I didn't!

BECCA

You were having sex with her boyfriend!

IZZY

That is so beside the point!

BECCA

It *is*?!

IZZY

It was over between them for a long time. They were just living together because of the rent situation. She didn't care what he did.

BECCA

Then why did she accost you in a crowded bar?

IZZY

Because she's a lunatic!

(Beat.)

And Auggie told her I was pregnant.

BECCA

Why would he—?

(Stops mid-sentence, then realizes . . .)

Oh my god, Izzy.

IZZY

I know, right?

BECCA

You are *not*.

(Izzy just shrugs "Whadaya gonna do?" Becca is not pleased.)

Oh my god.

IZZY

He's a really good guy, Bec. You're gonna like him. He's a musician.

BECCA

(Oozing irony) That's terrific.

IZZY

No, not like you think. He gets work. He's a *working* musician.

BECCA

Is that why you're here? To tell me you're pregnant?

IZZY

Pretty much.

BECCA

I knew something was up. You're not one to *pop* by on a Saturday afternoon.

IZZY

I pop by.

BECCA

How long have you known?

IZZY

A few weeks.

BECCA

And you're just telling me now?

IZZY

Well Jesus, Bec . . .

BECCA

What? You didn't wanna tell me?

IZZY

No.

BECCA

Why not?

IZZY

Why do you *think*?

(Beat.)

God, everything's so fucked-up.

BECCA

Does Mom know?

IZZY

Yeah.

BECCA

You told Mom before me?

IZZY

I *had* to.

BECCA

Oh my god, Izzy.

IZZY

Stop saying that.

BECCA

What are you gonna do?

IZZY

Well I'm gonna keep it, if that's what you're asking.

(Beat.)

Auggie wants to, too. We're excited about it. This is exactly the kind of thing that gives a person clarity.

(Beat.)

BECCA

Izzy . . .

IZZY

Look, I'm sure this is really hard for you, for a bunch of reasons, but can I just say . . . ? I don't need any advice right now. Or any lectures or whatever it is you're composing inside your head at the moment. I just need you to pretend to be happy for me. Okay? Even if you don't feel that right now. I'd like you to pretend that you do. All right?

(Pause.)

BECCA

Well . . . of *course* I'm happy for you. I was just taken aback. If you think a baby is gonna . . . fulfill you, or give you clarity or whatever, then, obviously it's a wonderful thing. I *am* happy for you. I don't need to *pretend*. Jesus, Izzy, gimme some credit.

(Izzy hugs her sister.)

IZZY

Thank you.

(Silence. Becca looks at the stacks of folded kids clothes.)

BECCA

Well I should probably hold off on this then.

IZZY

What do you mean?

BECCA

I'm washing all these clothes to give to Goodwill. I might as well save them for you. In case you have a boy. No sense in my giving these away.

(Izzy looks from Becca to the clothes. Piles of little pants and shirts and balled-up socks. They're all clothes a four year old might wear. Izzy looks uneasy.)

IZZY

I don't know, Bec. They're in baby clothes for so long, it'd be a few years before he could even fit into this stuff.

BECCA

It comes up very quickly. You wouldn't even believe it.

IZZY

Plus we don't have a lot of room to . . .

BECCA

That's okay. I'll keep them here. In the basement. You'll be happy I saved them.

IZZY

But what if it's a girl?

BECCA

Then I'll bring them down to Goodwill. What's the big deal? You're gonna thank me. A couple years worth of free clothes here. Think of the money you're gonna save.

IZZY

It's not about the money.

BECCA

Well it *should* be. You need to start thinking about stuff like that, Iz. Especially if the dad's a musician. It costs a lot to raise a child.

IZZY

It'd be weird, that's all. If it's a boy. To see him running around in Danny's clothes.

(Beat.)

I would feel weird. You would, too, I think.

(Beat.)

I'm sorry.

BECCA

No, *I'm* sorry. Of course it'd be weird. I don't know what I was—

IZZY

It was a nice offer. I just—

BECCA

You'll get a lot of clothes anyway. Christmas and birthdays. You won't have to worry about that.

IZZY

No I know but—

BECCA

It would be one thing if they were hand-me-downs but—

IZZY

Exactly.

(Pause. Becca goes back to folding.)

BECCA

It's probably a girl anyway.

IZZY

You think?

BECCA

I'm definitely getting a girl vibe. I'm a little psychic about this stuff.

IZZY

Oh yeah?

BECCA

Remember I said Debbie was having a girl.

IZZY

You did.

BECCA

And Karen?

IZZY

Karen too, I remember.

BECCA

I think there's a girl in there.

IZZY

I hope there is. That's what I want. I mean, either way, so long as it's healthy obviously, but if I had to pick, I hope it's a girl.

BECCA

Me, too.

(Beat.)

What'd Mom say?

IZZY

She was happy.

(Beat.)

BECCA

Really?

IZZY

I know. I thought she'd lay into me but . . .

BECCA

Huh.

(Becca clears Izzy's crème caramel plate, and brings it to the sink.)

IZZY

Thanks for the crème caramel.

BECCA

Sure.

(Beat.)

IZZY

I'm sorry, Bec. If this is hard. I know the timing really sucks.

BECCA

Hey. What can ya do?

(Beat.)

I'm glad you told me.

(Beat.)

And I'm really happy for you.

(The lights fade.)

Scene Two

Becca and Howie's living room, later that night. Dessert has moved in here. They're finishing up their crème caramels, chatting.

BECCA

Ridiculous, right? Nine weeks pregnant. In a bar. Drinking.

HOWIE

You said she *wasn't* drinking.

BECCA

No, *she* said. But you know Izzy. Plus the place was probably *clogged* with cigarette smoke.

HOWIE

Not anymore. Clean Indoor Air Act.

BECCA

She was in *Yonkers*. You think they enforce that in Yonkers?

HOWIE

I wouldn't worry about it. If the babies in France turn out okay, I'm sure this one'll be fine, too.

BECCA

You think this is funny, Howie?

HOWIE

Of course not. But you need to relax about it. Izzy could be right.

BECCA

About what?

HOWIE

The baby getting her on track. It can wake a person up. It did us.

BECCA

She was bragging about a *bar* fight.

HOWIE

It wasn't a bar fight.

BECCA

They were in a *bar*. *Fighting*.

HOWIE

Izzy hit someone, she didn't get into a fight. Blows were never exchanged.

BECCA

What is your point? It's okay for a pregnant woman to be punching people?

HOWIE

Well so long as they don't punch her back, it's probably all right.

BECCA

What are you—? Why are you defending her?

HOWIE

I'm not. I just think it's silly to get worked up about it.

BECCA

I'm not worked up. I'm just saying.

HOWIE

You're right, it's a mess, but what can we do? Maybe it'll be fine. Izzy's not a moron. *(Off her look)* Okay, she *acts* like one sometimes but . . . A baby can be good for a person.

BECCA

I know that, Howie.

HOWIE

All right then.

(Beat.)

This was good. The crème caramel.

BECCA

Thank you. Izzy tried to eat one upside down.

(Becca clears the crème caramel dishes. She brings them into the kitchen.)

HOWIE

You want more wine?

BECCA

(From the kitchen) No, I've had two already.

HOWIE

Half a glass, I wanna empty this bottle.

(He empties the rest into her glass.)

BECCA

Mom's thrilled by the way.

HOWIE

She called?

BECCA

Izzy must've told her I knew.

HOWIE

And how was that?

BECCA

What, two hours on the phone with *Mom*?

(Howie lowers the lights in the room as Becca reenters.)

What are you doing?

HOWIE

My eyes are sore, staring at that computer all day.

(Becca settles onto the couch with her wine.)

BECCA

You think this means she wants baby stuff? For her birthday? Maternity clothes or something?

HOWIE

(Joins her on the couch) No, wait for the baby shower. Just get whatever you were gonna get her.

BECCA

Good, because I was gonna buy her a bathroom set.

HOWIE

A what?

BECCA

A bathroom set. Shower curtain, bath mat . . . a little skirt for the sink. They sell them as sets.

HOWIE

This is for Izzy's birthday?

BECCA

The last time I was over there, you should've seen her bathroom. It looked like a frat boy decorated.

HOWIE

Huh.

BECCA

What?

HOWIE

It just seems like a funny gift. A bath mat.

BECCA

It's the whole set, Howie.

HOWIE

No, I know. Still.

BECCA

I thought it'd be nice.

HOWIE

It *is* nice. But maybe she'd rather have perfume or something.

BECCA

Izzy doesn't wear perfume.

HOWIE

No, I know, but—

BECCA

I was trying to be practical.

HOWIE

Okay.

BECCA

It's a good gift. I'd like it if someone gave it to me.

HOWIE

I'll make note of that for Christmas.

BECCA

You think it's dumb.

HOWIE

No, get her the sink skirt, the set-thingy whatever.

BECCA

Bathroom set.

HOWIE

Get her that if you think she'll like it.

BECCA

I'm gonna.

HOWIE

Great. She'll love it.

BECCA

You should've just said that to begin with.

HOWIE

Yeah, I know. Now.

(Howie looks at her and smiles. She smiles back. A moment passes between them.)

BECCA

How was squash?

HOWIE

Good. I lost but it was good.

BECCA

How's Rick?

HOWIE

Rick's fine.

BECCA

And Debbie?

HOWIE

Debbie wasn't there.

BECCA

I know, but did Rick mention her?

HOWIE

Not really. I guess she took the kids to her mother's this weekend.

BECCA

Rick didn't wanna go?

HOWIE

He has work.

BECCA

How *are* the kids?

HOWIE

Fine, I guess. He said that Robbie's doing T-ball now, and Emily has mastered the plié.

(Beat.)

Anything else?

BECCA

No, that's it.

HOWIE

You can call her, you know. You can call Debbie and ask her these questions yourself.

BECCA

I don't wanna call her. She should call me.

HOWIE

Okay.

BECCA

Why can't *she* call *me*?

HOWIE

I don't know.

BECCA

No?

HOWIE

She's uncomfortable, Bec.

BECCA

Is that what Rick said?

HOWIE

Rick didn't say anything. But obviously if she hasn't called you it's because she doesn't know what to say.

BECCA

How about, "Hey, Becca, how you doing? Haven't seen you in a while."

HOWIE

If you're pissed, you should call her and tell her.

BECCA

No, Howie, it's her job to call me.

HOWIE

Okay.

BECCA

I would've been there for her if god forbid something had ever happened to Robbie or Em. I wouldn't have vanished the way she did.

HOWIE

People get weird, you know that. It's probably hard for her.

BECCA

Hard for *her*?

HOWIE

I'm just saying. Look at my brother. Spent the whole funeral talking about the Mets. Obviously he couldn't deal. He'd talk about anything *but* Danny. And that's my brother.

BECCA

Yeah, well, your brother's an asshole.

(Beat.)

I should drop her a note.

HOWIE

Maybe you should.

BECCA

"Dear Debbie—just so's ya know, accidents aren't contagious."

HOWIE

Okay, let it go.

BECCA

Let what go?

HOWIE

Whatever's making you tense. You should try to relax a little.

BECCA

I *am* relaxed.

HOWIE

We'll see.

(Howie grabs a remote and clicks on the stereo. Al Green's "Livin' for You" plays quietly.)

BECCA

Oh jeez, Howie.

HOWIE

What? It's chill music. You need it. Now turn around.

BECCA

For what?

HOWIE

Just face that way.

(She does. He moves in to massage her shoulders.)

Thank you.

(Massages her) See? Your shoulders are all knotted-up.

BECCA

Yeah, well . . .

HOWIE

Forget about Debbie and Izzy and whoever else is bugging you.

BECCA

She has no idea, by the way. Izzy. *No* idea what she's getting into.

HOWIE

(Massaging her) I know.

BECCA

Do you remember how exhausted we were? The feedings at all hours. The sleep deprivation. Do you think Izzy's ready for that? The utter torture of it all?

HOWIE

Enough about Izzy.

BECCA

I'm sorry. But she's a sleeper. Izzy *needs* sleep more than other people. You talk about wake-up call or whatever you were saying, well she's gonna *get* one, big time.

(Howie continues to massage her. Becca seems to warm up to it.)

HOWIE

Maybe we should go somewhere. A cruise or something. You need to be pampered.

BECCA

You've taken off enough time as it is.

HOWIE

I'll talk to Alan. What's another week? I can handle most of my accounts from out of town anyway.

(He kisses her neck.)

BECCA

What are you doing?

HOWIE

I'm kissing your neck.

BECCA

Why?

HOWIE

I'm trying to relax you.

BECCA

Uh-huh.

HOWIE

Something wrong with that?

BECCA

I see what this is. Dimming the lights.

HOWIE

What? I can't massage my wife?

BECCA

(*Giggles a little*) You don't have eye strain.

HOWIE

So?

BECCA

"Oh I've been staring at that computer all day."

HOWIE

Well I *do* stare at that computer all day.

BECCA

You're trying to seduce me.

HOWIE

Am I?

BECCA

Plying me with liquor.

HOWIE

It worked in college.

BECCA

All right, Romeo.

HOWIE

What?

BECCA

(Pushing him away playfully) That's enough.

HOWIE

Why?

BECCA

You're being very naughty.

HOWIE

Naughty's good. You used to like naughty.

(She gets up from the couch.)

Where are you going?

BECCA

I still have stuff to bag up.

HOWIE

Are you kidding?

BECCA

No, there are piles of clothes up there, Howie.

HOWIE

Well if they've waited *this* long.

BECCA

I wanted to get it done.

HOWIE

We'll get it done tomorrow. I'll pitch in.

BECCA

Yeah, right.

HOWIE

I will.

BECCA

Uh-huh.

HOWIE

Becca . . .

BECCA

I'm sorry. I'm feeling kinda antsy tonight. You're right, the Izzy stuff got under my skin.

HOWIE

Right.

(He clicks the music off. Pause.)

BECCA

So, what, you're gonna pout now?

HOWIE

Well Jesus, Bec . . .

BECCA

Jesus, *what*?

HOWIE

It's been almost eight months.

(Beat.)

BECCA

But who's keeping track?

HOWIE

I am. I'm keeping track.

(Beat.)

I'm sorry. *(Off her look)* What? That makes me perverted? Wanting to have sex with my wife?

BECCA

I didn't say that.

HOWIE

Well you give me these looks like I should feel guilty.

BECCA

Funny, I've been getting the same looks from you.

HOWIE

When have I ever made you feel guilty?

BECCA

I'm just not ready yet, Howie. I'm sorry if you think that's abnormal.

HOWIE

I don't.

BECCA

Then what's the problem here?

HOWIE

We're *never* gonna be ready.

BECCA

If this is just about the sex, Howie—

HOWIE

It's not *just* about the sex.

BECCA

No, then what else is this?

HOWIE

It's also . . . about . . . I don't know. Maybe it *is* just the sex. I don't even know honestly. But we're not gonna suddenly wake up one day and be back where we were.

BECCA

I know that.

HOWIE

So we need to . . . head in that direction at least. Which will feel strange for a while, but . . .

BECCA

But you wanna have sex.

HOWIE

Don't say it like that.

BECCA

Why not?

HOWIE

Because it sounds crass and selfish.

BECCA

Well considering everything else—the fact that Danny died for example—don't you think maybe it *is* a little crass and selfish? For you to be roping me into sex when I don't wanna have it?

HOWIE

I wasn't *roping* you into anything. *Jesus.*

BECCA

No? Al Green isn't roping?

HOWIE

No.

BECCA

Al Green.

HOWIE

I thought it was nice. That's all. I was trying to make things nice.

BECCA

Well . . . you can't. I'm sorry. But things aren't "nice" anymore.

(Pause.)

HOWIE

I think you should see someone. I know you're not one for therapists, but I think you should. We could go together if that'd help. Or maybe you could try the group again.

BECCA

No.

HOWIE

There are a couple new parents now. It's changed the dynamic a little.

BECCA

We've had this discussion, Howie.

HOWIE

Fine, a psychiatrist then. Someone to talk to.

(Pause.)

No? Yes? Do you have an opinion?

BECCA

I think we should sell the house.

(Beat.)

HOWIE

Come on, Becca, what?

BECCA

I've been thinking about it for a while, and since we're on the topic—

HOWIE

How were we on the topic?

BECCA

I think it'd help if we moved.

HOWIE

I don't wanna move.

BECCA

He's everywhere, Howie. Everywhere I look, I still see Danny.

HOWIE

We love this house.

BECCA

I can't move without—I mean, Jesus, look at this. *(Grabs a spiky toy dinosaur from nearby) Everywhere*. Do you even *know*? *(Grabs a kids book from a stack of magazines)* Here: *Runaway Bunny* for godsake. The puzzles. The smudgy fingerprints on the doorjambs.

HOWIE

I like seeing his fingerprints.

BECCA

Because you don't have to sit and stare at them day in and day out. You get to escape. You get to go to work.

HOWIE

Well, if you want to go back to work, Becca—

BECCA

I don't.

HOWIE

—you can call up Sotheby's.

BECCA

No I can't. That's not who I am anymore. I left all that to be a mom.

HOWIE

Well . . .

BECCA

Well what? Well that didn't work out?

HOWIE

I didn't say that.

BECCA

Then what?

HOWIE

If that's the issue—

BECCA

If *what's* the issue?

HOWIE

—then . . . maybe we should try again.

(Beat.)

BECCA

Oh for godsakes, Howie . . .

HOWIE

What? I'm only saying.

BECCA

Is that . . . Is *that* what this was?

HOWIE

No. No, of course not. It just . . . it might be something to talk about at some point.

BECCA

I . . . I can't. I'm sorry. I can't have that talk.

HOWIE

Okay.

(They are silent, then Becca heads for the stairs. She stops and turns back.)

BECCA

Look maybe . . . maybe we can consider it at least. The house?

(Beat.)

HOWIE

Yeah. we'll consider it.

BECCA

Thank you.

(Becca heads upstairs with the dinosaur and the book. Howie watches her go. He sits alone for a couple beats. Then he gets up and goes to the TV cabinet. He rummages around quietly, looking through videotapes. He finally finds what he's looking for.

He glances up the stairs, then pops the video in. He shuts off the lights, then sits and watches, the light from the TV flickering on his face. He's watched this tape dozens of times. He doesn't tear up. He just watches it, occasionally smiling at something he hears. The volume is low, but we can hear some of it.)

VOICE OF DANNY

Now can I?

VOICE OF HOWIE

Let me just get the dog. Taz, lay down.

(On the video, we hear a dog barking and whining a little over this.)

VOICE OF DANNY

Ready?

VOICE OF HOWIE

Hold on. Taz, down!

VOICE OF DANNY

Lay down, Taz!

VOICE OF HOWIE

I got him. Quick now, before he gets up. Come on, come on . . .

(Danny comes running.)

Aaaaand . . .

VOICE OF DANNY

Geronimo!

VOICE OF HOWIE

Good job!

VOICE OF DANNY

Did you see me, Daddy?

VOICE OF HOWIE

I did.

VOICE OF DANNY

No you didn't. I'm invisible.

VOICE OF HOWIE

Ohhh.

(Becca's shadow appears at the top of the stairs, unseen by Howie. She listens for a couple beats.)

VOICE OF DANNY

I have magic.

VOICE OF HOWIE

Oh, I didn't realize.

VOICE OF DANNY

Do you wanna be invisible?

VOICE OF HOWIE

Okay.

VOICE OF DANNY

Pffffhhh.

VOICE OF HOWIE

Is that it? Am I invisible?

VOICE OF DANNY

Yeah. I made you invisible.

(Becca's shadow slips away from the stairs.)

VOICE OF HOWIE

Do you see me?

VOICE OF DANNY

Yeah.

VOICE OF HOWIE

No, you don't. I'm invisible.

VOICE OF DANNY

But I can still see you because I have magic.

VOICE OF HOWIE

Ohhh.

VOICE OF DANNY

Did you forget that part?

VOICE OF HOWIE

Yeah, I forgot that part.

(The lights fade on Howie, watching the video.)

Scene Three

The eat-in kitchen. A week later. Evening. Becca, Izzy and Nat, their mom, are gathered around a birthday cake singing "Happy Birthday." Nat has a glass of wine.

NAT AND BECCA

(End of the song) "Happy birthday, dear Isabel . . . Happy birthday to you . . ."

NAT

Blow 'em out.

(Izzy blows out the candles. Ad-lib yays and clapping. Becca goes to get a knife.)

BECCA

What'd you wish for?

IZZY

I can't *say.*

(Regarding the cake) It looks good, Becca.

NAT

Where'd you buy it?

BECCA

I didn't. I made it.

NAT

Of course you did. What a stupid question. Of course you made it.

BECCA

(Catches Izzy scooping off the frosting) Izzy—

IZZY

It's *my* cake.

BECCA

Well let me cut it first. Watch your fingers.

(Becca cuts slices of cake and puts them on plates over the following. Howie enters with a couple papers.)

HOWIE

You didn't wait for me?

BECCA

You said not to.

HOWIE

I didn't *mean* it though.

NAT

I tried to stop them, Howie.

IZZY

I wanted cake.

HOWIE

Rude.

BECCA

I didn't know how long you were gonna be up there. Once you get on that computer . . .

NAT

Did you get it?

HOWIE

Yeah, right here. *(Hands her papers)*

NAT

Let me get my glasses. *(Gets her glasses from her purse)*

BECCA

(To Howie) Did you have to?

HOWIE

She wanted me to look it up.

BECCA

Any excuse to escape for ten minutes.

IZZY

(Regarding Nat) Well do you blame him?

NAT

(Regarding printout) What *is* this?

IZZY

Mom, cake.

HOWIE

It's a timeline, starting with the lobotomy. The plane crashes. It's the whole list. It's long.

NAT

Well still, that doesn't make it a curse.

BECCA

Nobody said it was a curse, Mother.

NAT

Everybody says. That was my point. *Everybody* says it's a curse.

BECCA

Well nobody in this room.

NAT

You know what it is, really? Hype. Perpetuating the myth. That whole American royalty crap.

IZZY

It's good cake.

NAT

But the Kennedys aren't cursed. They're just really unlucky. And kinda stupid, a lot of them.

HOWIE

Cut me a piece, wouldja Bec?

NAT

Too much money, that's their curse. And too much time on their hands. If they had to go to work, like normal people, then most of those Kennedys would still be alive.

IZZY

Thanks, Howie. I'm so glad you went and got that timeline.

NAT

Maybe if they had stayed home and watched television once in a while, instead of zipping off to Vail, then none of that stuff would've happened.

BECCA

You have the most interesting theories.

NAT

Don't patronize me.

BECCA

I'm not. I was being serious.

IZZY

(Regarding cake) This is so good.

NAT

Normal people don't fly around in their own planes for example. I don't know anyone with his own plane, do you? Do you, Howie?

HOWIE

Well, yeah I know *one* guy but—

NAT

Well, *you* know someone, but that's not the norm. An average person doesn't own an airplane.

HOWIE

No, you're right, he's not average.

BECCA

He's a member of the jet set.

NAT

Exactly! That's what that word means! The jet set. Jet-setters! Buzzing around in little Pipers or whatever, crashing off the coast of Massachusetts. Regular people don't have ten relatives die in separate plane wrecks.

HOWIE

It's not ten.

NAT

Just about, if you count Teddy who survived his.

IZZY

Well I think it's sad.

BECCA

Teddy surviving?

NAT

Well of course it's *sad*. All those good-looking people falling out of the sky like that. It's a frickin' waste. But it isn't a curse. It's just rich people acting stupid.

BECCA

I thought you liked JFK?

NAT

I'm not talking about JFK. I'm not talking about the ones who were *assassinated*. Although getting shot by a crazed gunman is kinda a rich-guy problem too, isn't it?

HOWIE

Well, not *necessarily*.

NAT

It doesn't matter, that's not who I'm talking about. I'm talking about the unqualified *pilots*. I'm talking about playing football. And skiing. At the *same* time!

IZZY

That *was* stupid.

NAT

"Hey, look at me! I'm a Kennedy! I can catch a ball while flying down a mountain on sticks!" Of *course* he died. Idiot. And I know that's a terrible thing to say, but this was a grown man acting like a moron. The arrogance of these people.

HOWIE

The Greeks would call that hubris. "Arrogance in the face of . . ." It might not technically be hubris actually.

NAT

If hubris means reckless, then that's right.

HOWIE

No, it doesn't mean reckless. It's more about the gods.

NAT

That's probably the right word then. They're *very* Catholic, those Kennedys.

HOWIE

Now I'm curious, I'm gonna look it up. *(Goes to find dictionary)*

NAT

(Regarding wine bottle) Fill me up, wouldja Becca?

(Becca reluctantly refills her glass.)

Isn't this nice? Sitting around talking politics? I never do this. It's a nice change.

(Becca turns to pour Izzy some wine. Izzy puts her hand over the glass.)

IZZY

It's juice. I'm drinking juice.

BECCA

Right, sorry.

IZZY

That's the third time you've done that.

BECCA

I know, I'm sorry.

IZZY

Are you testing me, Becca?

BECCA

No, I'm not testing you. It's just habit. I'm sorry.

HOWIE

(With dictionary) Here it is: "hubris, an insolent pride or presumption."

NAT

That's them all right. Insolent pride.

HOWIE

And number two is: "in Greek tragedy, arrogance toward the gods leading to nemesis."

IZZY

It's like coming to school when we visit you two.

HOWIE

Is that right?

BECCA

Izzy hated school.

IZZY

No, I didn't. Don't listen to her, Howie. I liked school. Just because I was lousy at it didn't mean I hated it.

BECCA

Sounds like you and squash, Howie.

HOWIE

(To Izzy) She means the game, not the vegetable.

IZZY

I knew what she meant.

NAT

You know who *was* cursed? *Rose* Kennedy. A hundred and four years old. Living through all that death, one after another. *She's* the one I feel sorry for.

(Beat.)

BECCA

Anyone want more cake?

HOWIE

None for me.

BECCA

We should do gifts then.

IZZY

Yay! Gifts!

NAT

I don't know how I got on all that Kennedy stuff. What was I talking about before?

HOWIE

Aristotle Onassis.

NAT

Oh right, that makes sense. What was I saying about him?

IZZY

You were saying how he'd get really tipsy and never stop talking.

NAT

(Laughs) You bitch. I'm not tipsy. I'm sure I had a very interesting point to make.

(Becca hands a big present to Izzy.)

BECCA

This is from us.

IZZY

Wow. Thank you.

HOWIE

Happy birthday.

IZZY

It's wrapped so nice. It's a shame to rip it open.

NAT

Becca always makes such nice bows. I don't have the patience. My fingers are too fat.

(Izzy unwraps a very tasteful bathroom set.)

Ohh, look at that.

BECCA

It's more of a practical gift, but I thought you could use it.

HOWIE

It's a bathroom set.

IZZY

I see. It's nice.

NAT

Look at the colors. So pretty.

BECCA

The gift receipt's inside if you want a different style.

NAT

Why would she want a different style? It's beautiful. Isn't it beautiful?

IZZY

Is this your way of telling me you don't like my Three Stooges shower curtain?

BECCA

Of course not.

IZZY

Okay.

BECCA

This is for when you want a change, you'll have it.

NAT

That Three Stooges thing *is* kinda goofy, honey.

IZZY

The word is kitschy, Mother.

NAT

Look up kitschy, wouldja Howie? See if it says crap?

BECCA

I didn't know what to get you.

IZZY

This is great. Seriously, thank you.

BECCA

I *like* your shower curtain.

IZZY

I know, I was kidding.

NAT

And since you're moving in with Auggie—

IZZY

That's right. His bathroom needs a little froofing up. Thank you.

BECCA

You're welcome.

IZZY

Thanks, Howie.

HOWIE

(Chuckles a little) Don't thank me. Becca picked it out. *(Off Becca's look)* What?

NAT

Okay, now me. *(Hands Izzy an envelope)*

IZZY

Oooh, an envelope. Smells like cash.

NAT

You *wish*. You think I'm gonna trust you with cash? It's a gift certificate.

IZZY

(Opens it) To A Pea in the Pod!

NAT

They have very nice maternity clothes. Nothing schlubby.

IZZY

Thank you, Mommy. *(Hugs her)*

(Beat.)

BECCA

I thought we weren't doing baby stuff.

NAT

Who said that?

BECCA

For the birthday. I thought we'd wait until the shower.

NAT

I'll get her something else for the shower. What's the difference?

BECCA

Nothing, I just would've gotten her something different had I known we were doing baby stuff.

HOWIE

That's my fault. I told her to—

NAT

It's *not* baby stuff, it's mommy stuff. She's gonna need clothes.

BECCA

I know, that's why—

IZZY

This is perfect, Bec. I needed a bathroom set.

BECCA

I know you did, but you need baby stuff more.

HOWIE

So take it back. We can take it back.

IZZY

Don't tell her that.

BECCA

No, he's right. I should.

IZZY

Becca, please.

BECCA

I'll get you a basket of Mustela lotions instead. They prevent stretch marks.

(Becca tries to take the bathroom set back. She and Izzy struggle over it for a beat.)

IZZY

Becca, *let go*. I *like* the bathroom set. You can get the lotions another time.

(Becca lets go, a little embarrassed.)

BECCA

Okay.

IZZY

Thank you.

NAT

It's a nice set. I like the colors.

HOWIE

More juice, Izzy?

IZZY

No, I'm good.

(They sit in silence for a couple beats.)

NAT

So can anyone use those stretch-mark lotions, or just pregnant ladies?

HOWIE

Hey, how's Taz.

NAT

He's good. The vet says he needs to lose some weight though.

HOWIE

Really?

NAT

Yeah, he eats like a trooper.

HOWIE

What are you feeding him?

NAT

Just regular dog food. Whatever's on sale.

HOWIE

Oh. Because I wrote down the name of what he usually eats on that printout I gave you. Do you still have that printout?

NAT

Yeah.

HOWIE

We were feeding him Science Diet. They have this special low-fat mix.

NAT

Oh that stuff's so expensive though. He likes what I've been giving him.

HOWIE

Except it makes him fat.

BECCA

Howie—

NAT

He's not fat. He's just a little chubbier.

IZZY

I think the weight suits him.

NAT

Maybe he eats too much because he feels punished. That's what *I* do.

(Beat.)

I think he misses you.

IZZY

Remember Pickles? Now *she* was fat. *(To Howie)* That was our dog growing up. She was this enormous . . . I don't even *know* what. *(To Becca)* What breed was Pickles?

BECCA

She was a mutt.

IZZY

No, I know, but she was mostly collie I think, with some German shepherd mixed in. Remember how fat she was?

HOWIE

Probably because of what you fed her.

IZZY

Well, yeah, probably.

NAT

Now I remember what it was. What I was gonna say about Aristotle Onassis.

IZZY

Mom, do you have to—?

NAT

It was about his son, the one who died in the plane crash.

BECCA

I'm gonna wrap up the cake for you. *(She does)*

NAT

I know—another rich kid in a plane crash—but this was my whole point. You should've stopped me from going off on that Kennedy tangent, because my point was about Onassis, and how when his son died, he was so distraught by the senselessness of it all, that he put up this big reward to anyone who could prove that someone had sabotaged the plane. Have you read this, Howie?

HOWIE

I'm not sure.

NAT

He just couldn't accept that what had happened was an accident, so he offered all this money to anyone who could give him a reasonable explanation. He needed someone to blame.

BECCA

(To herself, while wrapping the cake) Aw, Jesus. Here we go.

NAT

He needed a *reason* for losing his son. But it didn't come of course. And it killed him. The grief did. He only lasted a couple years after that. Because he never came to terms with it. There was nothing to give him comfort, and so he died. You see?

(Becca turns to face her.)

He would rather his son have been killed by some kind of secret assassination than by bad luck. It's like the Kennedy curse, isn't it? People want things to make sense.

BECCA

We don't think Danny died because of a curse, Mom.

NAT

Of course not.

BECCA

Or because someone sabotaged us, or was out to get us. We know there's no sensible explanation.

NAT

I know you do.

BECCA

Then why are you telling this story?

NAT

I'm just talking. I can't talk?

BECCA

You never *just talk*. It *sounds* like you're just talking but it's always so much more, isn't it.

NAT

I don't even know what that means.

IZZY

Hey, here's an idea, let's change the subject.

BECCA

(To Howie) Didn't I say no wine?

HOWIE

She brought it herself, what was I supposed to do?

NAT

What'd I say?

IZZY

Mom, you promised.

NAT

Promised what? It's not my fault she missed my point.

BECCA

What point? That Aristotle Onassis died of grief because he couldn't find someone to *blame*?

NAT

I'm not talking about blame, I'm talking about comfort.

BECCA

Ohhh, comfort. Well then.

IZZY

You guys, this is supposed to be my party.

NAT

Where are you getting it?

BECCA

Comfort?

NAT

Yes, if I may ask.

BECCA

I'm not.

NAT

Well.

BECCA

Well what?

NAT

Well I think you should.

BECCA

Okay. I'll get right on that then. See what I can dig up on eBay.

NAT

Don't get flip, Becca. I'm just trying to talk to you.

IZZY

I'm gonna clean up, because I think we're just about done here.

NAT

Howie says you won't go to the support group.

(Beat.)

BECCA

Oh. Howie said.

HOWIE

She was asking how you were doing.

BECCA

Why didn't you just say fine? You know she's gonna run with whatever you give her.

NAT

I always thought talk was healthy. Isn't that what all the books say, Howie?

BECCA

So this is what exactly, an intervention?

IZZY

If it is, then I'm really pissed.

HOWIE

It's not an intervention.

NAT

We're just having a discussion.

IZZY

You couldn't wait until tomorrow? It had to happen on my birthday?

HOWIE

Izzy, please.

NAT

I remember when Arthur died, I found the support group very helpful.

BECCA

Well that's you. It isn't me. And Arthur isn't Danny.

NAT

I'm not saying he is. I'm just saying it was helpful.

HOWIE

She doesn't like the people.

BECCA

Howie—

HOWIE

What? You *don't*. I was just explaining.

NAT

What's wrong with the people? They've lost children, too. They understand what you're going through.

BECCA

No they don't. They understand what *they're* going through.

NAT

Still, you must have things in common.

BECCA

You would think so, Mother, but actually we don't. Other than that dead kid thing, of course.

NAT

It can't hurt to give it another try, Becca.

BECCA

Actually, it *can*. You haven't met that room full of God-freaks.

HOWIE

They're not God-freaks.

BECCA

Most of them *are*, Howie. That's all they talk about. God's plan. "At least he's in a better place."

HOWIE

They're not all like that.

BECCA

My favorite is: "God needed another angel." What is *that*? He's *God*! Why can't he just *make* another angel? These people . . .

NAT

Maybe God gives them comfort.

BECCA

Well it pisses me off. Trying to find some ridiculous meaning in— "Hey look, I stepped in shit, it must be part of God's plan."

NAT

Now you're just being silly.

BECCA

I'm being silly.

NAT

Faith helps people cope. What's wrong with that? I know when your brother died—

BECCA

Again with Arthur.

NAT

If I didn't have God—

BECCA

See? That's *exactly* why I don't go: "If I didn't have God."

HOWIE

They're not all like that. Kevin's not. Gabby's not like that.

NAT

It sounds like you're jealous of their comfort.

BECCA

Yes, I *am*. Of *course* I am. How nice they all have something that makes them feel a little better. Like I don't feel bad enough, I've gotta go and have *that* rubbed in my face?

HOWIE

Nobody's rub— You're not being fair.

NAT

I don't know why you don't believe in God anyway.

BECCA

(To Howie) You see? *Now* look where we're going!

NAT

I brought you to church every Sunday. You *used* to believe in God.

BECCA

Well I don't anymore.

NAT

Well you should. What if you're wrong? What if there *is* a God?

BECCA

Then I would say he's a sadistic prick.

IZZY	NAT	HOWIE
Whoa, hey now . . .	Becca, please.	Aw, jeez . . .

BECCA

"Worship me and I'll treat you like shit." No wonder you like him, he sounds just like Dad.

NAT

You don't need to strike out at me, Becca. I know you're still in a bad place, but I'm trying to help you.

BECCA

Right.

NAT

I wish someone had sat me down when Arthur died. I wish someone gave me a little advice.

BECCA

You know what *I* wish?! *I* wish you would stop comparing Danny to Arthur! *Danny* was a four-year-old boy who chased his dog into the street! *Arthur* was a thirty-year-old *heroin* addict who *hung* himself! Frankly I resent how you keep lumping them together.

(Silence.)

NAT

He was still my son.

BECCA

And I don't recall anyone giving you instructions on how best to grieve for him.

(Beat.)

I think it's time for me to go to bed now.

(Turns to her sister) Izzy, I hope you enjoy the bathroom set.

IZZY

I'm gonna.

(Becca heads upstairs. Izzy loads the dishwasher. Nat is still shaken by Becca's comment.)

NAT

I was never that mean to anyone. When Arthur died, I was just as upset as she was, but I never took it out on other people like that.

IZZY

What about Mrs. Bailey?

NAT

(Turns to her, annoyed) Nobody's talking about Mrs. Bailey. Izzy, please.

HOWIE

You know what this was about?

IZZY

Yeah, *her* and her mouth.

HOWIE

I knew the party was a bad idea.

IZZY

(To Nat) Didn't I tell you not to get into anything with her?

HOWIE

We got a letter today. From Jason Willette.

(Beat.)

NAT

What, why? What'd he want?

HOWIE

She said it didn't bother her but . . .
(Regarding the gathering) Sorry, Iz.

IZZY

No, hey, this was *great*, really. Let's do it again *next* year.

(Crossfade to:)

Scene Four

Later that night. Lights up on Danny's room. It looks essentially the same as it did when Danny was alive.

The door opens and Becca enters. She doesn't come in here often. She quietly closes the door behind her. She looks around a bit, then takes a seat on Danny's bed. She takes a letter out of an envelope and rereads it.

Lights up on Jason Willette, seventeen.

JASON

Dear Mr. and Mrs. Corbett,

I wanted to send you my condolences on the death of your son, Danny. I know it's been eight months since the accident, but I'm sure it's probably still hard for you to be reminded of that day. I think about what happened a lot, as I'm sure you do, too. I've been having some troubles at home, and at school, and a couple people here thought it might be a good idea to write to you. I'm sorry if this letter upsets you. That's obviously not my intention.

Even though I never knew Danny, I did read that article in the town paper, and was happy to learn a little bit about him. He sounds like he was a great kid. I'm sure you miss him a lot, as you said in the article. I especially liked the part where Mr. Corbett talked about Danny's robots, because when I was his age I was a big fan of robots, too. In fact I still am, in some ways—ha ha.

I've enclosed a short story that's going to be printed in my high school lit magazine. I don't know if you like science fiction or not, but I've enclosed it anyway. I was hoping to dedicate the story to Danny's memory. There aren't any robots in this one, but I think it would be the kind of story he'd like if he were my age. Would it bother you if I dedicated the story? If so, please let me know. The printer deadline for the magazine is March 31st. If you tell me before then, I can have them take it off.

(Becca flips through the story enclosed.)

I know this probably doesn't make things any better, but I wanted you to know how terrible I feel about Danny. I know that no matter how hard this has been on me, I can never understand the depth of your loss. My mom has only told me that about a hundred times—ha ha. I of course wanted to say how sorry I am that things happened the way they did, and that I wish I had driven down a different block that day. I'm sure you do, too.

Anyway, that's it for now. If you'd like to let me know about the dedication, you can email me at the address above. If I don't hear from you, I'll assume it's okay.

Sincerely, Jason Willette

(Beat.)

P.S. Would it be possible to meet you in person at some point?

(The lights slowly fade on Jason.

Becca puts the story and letter aside. She just sits on the bed, taking in the room.

Meanwhile, the lights rise on Howie in the living room. It's that same night. Nat and Izzy have gone home. Howie plunks into his chair and grabs a couple remotes. He clicks on the TV, then hits play on the VCR. We hear a documentary on tornadoes playing. Howie is confused. Something isn't right.

He gets out of the chair and ejects the tape. He examines the tape, panic starts to set in. He pops the tape back in and hits play again. More tornado documentary.)

HOWIE

What is this? Becca? . . . Becca?!

(He hits fast forward.)

Becca?!

BECCA

(From upstairs) What?

HOWIE

What'd you do here?!

(The lights fade on Danny's bedroom.

Howie keeps pressing fast forward, but it's all tornadoes. He's beside himself. Becca comes running downstairs.)

BECCA

What's the matter?!

HOWIE

What is this?!

BECCA

What's *what*?!

HOWIE

The *television*. What *is* this?

BECCA

(Looks to TV) It's the Discovery Channel. The tornado program. You said you wanted to watch it. I recorded it for you. Why?

HOWIE

For *chrissake*!

BECCA

What's the matter?

HOWIE

It's Danny's tape. You recorded over Danny's tape.

(Beat.)

BECCA

No, I didn't. *Pride and Prejudice* was on that tape. We were watching it last night.

HOWIE

I switched them.

BECCA

What?!

HOWIE

I watched Danny's tape later. After you went to bed.

BECCA

Why didn't you take it out of the machine?!

HOWIE

Why didn't you check to see what was in there?!

BECCA

I assumed it was the TV tape!

HOWIE

Jesus, Becca!

BECCA

It was one of the baby videos?

HOWIE

No, it was the most recent, the long one. The park was on it, and Mexico—

BECCA

How was I supposed to know you snuck down here?

HOWIE

—and Christmas.

BECCA

I thought it was the TV tape.

HOWIE

It wasn't!

BECCA

I know, Howie.

HOWIE

So it's gone. The whole thing.

BECCA

I'm sorry.

HOWIE

It's the only copy, Becca!

BECCA

Well, I didn't do it on purpose.

HOWIE

Are ya sure?

(Beat.)

BECCA

What does that mean?

(No response.)

You think I recorded over Danny's tape on purpose?

HOWIE

I don't know.

BECCA

You don't *know*?

HOWIE

I should've taken it out.

BECCA

Why would I deliberately record over it?

HOWIE

I don't know.

BECCA

Why *would* I?!

HOWIE

I don't *know*!

(Silence.)

You took the paintings off the fridge. Danny's paintings.

BECCA

To save them. I put them in plastic.

HOWIE

And shoved them in a box.

BECCA

For safekeeping.

HOWIE

Okay.

BECCA

I didn't throw the paintings out.

HOWIE

I know you didn't.

BECCA

You think I didn't want that tape?

HOWIE

I don't— . . . Of course, you did. Obviously it wasn't on purpose but—

BECCA

What?

HOWIE

Maybe subconsciously.

BECCA

Subconsciously. Is this what they're telling you at group? How I'm doing things subconsciously?

HOWIE

You're trying to get rid of him. I'm sorry, but that's how it feels to me sometimes. Every day, it's something else. It feels like you're trying to get rid of any evidence he was ever here.

(It's as if she's been slapped.)

BECCA

I didn't know that tape was in there.

HOWIE

I'm not talking about the tape. Not just the tape.

BECCA

And the paintings are downstairs. In a box. You can look at them whenever you want.

HOWIE

The clothes. His shoes.

BECCA

We don't need all that stuff. Why would we keep—?

HOWIE

Your wanting to sell the house!

BECCA

We already talked about—

HOWIE

Taz. Sending Taz to your mother's!

BECCA

There was a lot going on, Howie. We couldn't deal with the dog.

HOWIE

I was fine with the dog. *I* was the one walking him.

BECCA

Well he got underfoot.

HOWIE

And he was a reminder.

BECCA

Yes, he was a reminder. So what? I wanted one less reminder around here. That's perfectly normal.

HOWIE

And since you never wanted the dog to begin with—

BECCA

Oh for godsakes—

HOWIE

Well if I hadn't bought the dog—

BECCA

And if *I* hadn't run inside to get the phone, or if *I* had latched the gate—

HOWIE

I left the gate unlatched!

BECCA

Well *I* didn't check it!

(Retreats a bit) I'm not playing this game again, Howie. It was no one's fault.

HOWIE

Not even the dog's.

BECCA

I *know* that.

HOWIE

Dogs chase squirrels. Boys chase dogs.

BECCA

Are you telling me or yourself?

HOWIE

He *loved* that dog!

BECCA

Of course he did.

HOWIE

And you got rid of him!

BECCA

Right, like I got rid of the tape. I get it.

HOWIE

(Losing it) It's not just the tape! I'm not talking about the tape, Becca! It's Taz, and the paintings, and the clothes, and it's *everything*! You have to stop erasing him! You have to stop it! You HAVE TO STOP!

(Howie has been reduced to tears. He has to move away from Becca. She takes him in. She seems more confused than affronted.)

BECCA

Do you really not know me, Howie? Do you really not know how utterly impossible that would be? To erase him? No matter how many things I give to charity, or how many art projects I box up, do you really think I don't see him every second of every day? And okay, I'm trying to make things a little easier on myself by hiding some of the photos, and giving away the clothes, but that does *not* mean I'm trying to *erase* him. That tape was an accident. And believe me, I will beat myself up about it forever, I'm sure. Like everything else that I could've prevented but didn't.

HOWIE

That's not what I want, Bec. It's not what I'm talking about.

BECCA

No? Because it feels like it is. It feels like I don't feel bad enough for you. I'm not mourning enough for your taste.

HOWIE

Come on, that's not—

BECCA

Or mourning in the right *way*. But let me just say, Howie, that I am mourning as much as you are. And my grief is just as real and awful as yours.

HOWIE

I know that.

BECCA

You're not in a better place than I am, you're just in a *different* place. And that sucks that we can't be there for each other right now, but that's just the way it is.

HOWIE

His stuff is all we have left. That's all I'm saying. And every bit of it you get rid of—

BECCA

I understand that. You don't wanna let go of it. I understand, Howie.

HOWIE

Do you?

(Beat.)

Do you?

(No response.)

This isn't . . . —Something has to change here. Because I can't do this . . . like this. It's too hard.

(Beat.)

It's too hard.

(Neither speaks for a while. Then Howie heads for the stairs. He stops, and turns back to her.)

And I want that dog back. Your mother's making him fat.

(Beat.)

I want the dog back.

BECCA

Why don't we wait until—

HOWIE

I don't want to. How much more do we have to lose?

(Beat.)

I miss the dog. I'm sorry, but I miss him. I want him back.

(They regard each other silently. Howie heads upstairs, leaving Becca alone.

The lights slowly fade.)

Act Two

Scene One

Living room. We hear a car pulling away as the lights rise on Howie, standing by the open front door, in a suit jacket, holding a clipboard for an open house.

Two months have passed. It's early May. Izzy comes from the kitchen with a piece of torte. Her pregnancy is starting to show a little. She's four and a half months along.

IZZY

They were weird, huh? That last couple? The way they kept opening everything? Cabinets, closets . . .

HOWIE

It's an open house.

IZZY

Still, it was kinda nervy. I'd never do one of these things. Strangers strolling through, looking under my beds.

HOWIE

That's what you gotta do to sell a house.

IZZY

Well lucky for me I'll never own a house then.
(Regarding torte) What is this, pie?

HOWIE

It's a torte.

IZZY

Is it good?

HOWIE

Yeah, it's good.

(Izzy settles in with the torte.)

IZZY

We done?

HOWIE

Fifteen minutes. We're supposed to go till four. *(Looking over the sign-in sheet)*

IZZY

How many'd ya get anyway?

HOWIE

Not many. No *serious* buyers. Maybe the German though. It's hard to tell.

IZZY

Is that what he was, German? I couldn't place the accent. I thought maybe Irish.

HOWIE

Irish?

IZZY

I couldn't tell.

HOWIE

We should probably get a broker. I think a lot of people are afraid of fisbos.

IZZY

Afraida who?

HOWIE

Fisbo: For Sale By Owner. No middleman. I was trying to avoid the commission but we probably need one.

(Regarding sign-in sheet) This was a wash I think. *(Looking over clipboard)* I thought we had a bite with that family—the little girl. Nothing though. Maybe I priced it too high. Or they were just browsing maybe.

IZZY

(Eating) You freaked them out, Howie.

(Beat.)

HOWIE

No, I didn't. What are you talking about?

IZZY

You should've cleaned out Danny's room. Made it look like a guest room or something. An office, or whatever.

HOWIE

Why?

IZZY

Because everyone that went in there was like, "Oh, you have a son, how old is he?" Did you think people wouldn't ask that?

HOWIE

I didn't think about it. I just thought it'd be good for them to see there was a nice room for a kid.

IZZY

But common sense, Howie. You've got these robot sheets on the bed, the conversation's gonna come up. And so everyone asks, and then you tell them, and then there's this weirdness in the air.

HOWIE

Only *two* people asked. That's all.

IZZY

Well you ooged them out. If you had a kid, would you wanna move into a house where a boy just died? People believe in that stuff, you know. House karma, or whatever you wanna call it.

HOWIE

Well they're stupid then.

IZZY

Yeah, they are. But if you wanna sell your house you gotta take that into consideration. I can't believe *I'm* giving *you* business advice.

HOWIE

Is that what this is?

IZZY

I'm just saying, sometimes you gotta sort out what is and isn't appropriate to say to people.

HOWIE

It isn't appropriate to talk about my son?

IZZY

Uh-uh, you're not pulling me into that conversation. You wanna tell total strangers all about Danny and how he died, it's none of my business. God knows it's something you enjoy doing, so you go ahead. But don't be surprised if nobody wants to buy your house.

(Finishes torte) Good god, Becca has gotta stop baking. I'm gynormous.

(We hear the dog barking out in the yard. Howie looks outside.)

Someone coming?

HOWIE

(Regarding Taz) No, he's just mad he's still tied up.

IZZY

(Looks at her watch, then) So, hey, let me ask you something . . .

(Beat.)

HOWIE

All right.

IZZY

Why is Becca so mad at me? Is it just because I'm pregnant or . . .

HOWIE

Becca's not mad at you.

IZZY

Then why does she act so pissed at me sometimes?

HOWIE

I don't know. You should ask her.

IZZY

I can't.

HOWIE

Why not?

IZZY

Because that'll only make her *more* pissed.

HOWIE

Yeah, probably, but—

IZZY

Is it because she blames me? A little bit maybe?

HOWIE

Oh my god, Izzy . . .

IZZY

Because if I hadn't called to bitch about Mom she wouldn't have left Danny to run in to—

HOWIE

Ten months later and you're asking me this?

IZZY

Well, I don't know.

HOWIE

No, Izzy. No. Nobody blames you.

IZZY

Okay.

(Beat.)

So it's just the baby then. The fact that I'm having a baby.

HOWIE

Honestly, I don't think Becca's mood has anything to do with you.

IZZY

She thinks I can't do it. Right? I'm not cut out to be a good mother?

HOWIE

She doesn't think that. You should *really* be having this conversation with her.

IZZY

I know I've been a fuck-up, but people get their shit together.

HOWIE

Of course they do.

IZZY

And maybe I'm not as organized as Becca, or homey, or whatever—

HOWIE

Nobody's comparing you.

IZZY

Really? Because that'd be a first.

HOWIE

Everyone's excited about the baby, Iz. But you gotta understand that there's other stuff going on around here.

IZZY

I'm not talking about the other stuff. I'm talking about me being a capable person who can raise a child, and look after it and protect it. I resent the feeling I get from her, and you too sometimes, honestly, that I don't *deserve* the baby. Or that I'm not mature enough, or smart enough or something, to take care of it. I mean, my god, if my mother could do it, how hard could it be?

(Beat.)

HOWIE

You'd be surprised.

IZZY

Hey, that's not what I . . . I just want to feel like you guys have some faith in me, because I'm up to it.

HOWIE

Great. I hope you are.

IZZY

Oh, you *hope*. Thanks, Howie.

HOWIE

I don't know where you want this conversation to go. And I really don't know why you're having it with me.

(Glances at his watch) Aw fuck it. Nobody's coming.

(Howie takes off his suit jacket. He tosses it onto the couch, then heads into the kitchen.)

IZZY

Are you mad?

HOWIE

No.

IZZY

You seem mad.

HOWIE

(From kitchen) I'm just getting a beer. You want one?

IZZY

No, I don't want a beer. *God*.

(Howie gets himself a beer out of the fridge, then reenters from the kitchen.)

Can I ask you something else?

HOWIE

What do you got, a list? "Things to ask Howie when he's cornered?"

IZZY

No. Not a *list*.

HOWIE

What is it?

IZZY

You're not gonna like it.

HOWIE

Well then, even better.

IZZY

Do you know my friend Reema?

HOWIE

This is the question?

IZZY

No, this is the prologue. You know how some books have prologues?

HOWIE

I'm familiar with the concept.

IZZY

That's Reema. You remember her?

HOWIE

Not really.

IZZY

I brought her to that barbecue like two years ago? Curly hair, kinda chubby.

HOWIE

Okay. I'll take your word for it.

IZZY

Well, Reema works at Calderone's. In New Rochelle. You know that restaurant?

(Beat.)

HOWIE

Yeah.

IZZY

Well Reema, even though you don't remember her, remembers you pretty well from the barbecue, and she said she waited on you a couple weeks ago.

HOWIE

Did I stiff her on the tip? Because had I remembered her, obviously I would've—

IZZY

She said you were with a woman.

(Beat.)

HOWIE

I was with another parent from the support group. Two weeks ago, right? We grabbed a bite after the meeting. If Reema had identified herself, I would've introduced them.

IZZY

Her husband doesn't attend the meetings?

HOWIE

Is this still part of the prologue?

IZZY

Why were you holding hands?

(Beat.)

Reema said you were holding hands.

HOWIE

And Reema's what exactly, your spy?

IZZY

No, she's a waitress. She was just at work. *You* were the one sneaking around.

HOWIE

Okay, now I *am* mad.

IZZY

I told you, you weren't gonna like it.

HOWIE

That woman is a friend of mine whose daughter died of leukemia six months ago. Jesus, Izzy, what are you trying to—?

IZZY

I'm just asking a question. You don't have to get defensive.

HOWIE

Just because I was holding a person's hand doesn't mean—

IZZY

I know you and Becca are having troubles—

HOWIE

What are you *talking* about?

IZZY

—but I'd like to think that if things got to a point where they were unsavable, that you'd be man enough to fish or cut bait—

HOWIE

Who said we were having troubles?

IZZY

—and not make things worse than they already are by fucking around behind Becca's back.

HOWIE

You are *way* off base, Izzy!

IZZY

And I know there's "other stuff going on around here" but that doesn't excuse it.

HOWIE

This is so beyond ridiculous, I don't even know how to respond to you.

IZZY

I don't need you to respond. I just wanted to ask the question and say what I had to say. You can do whatever you want about it.

HOWIE

About *what*? I'm not having an affair!

IZZY

Okay.

HOWIE

I was comforting a friend!

IZZY

Great, I'm glad to hear that.

HOWIE

And I don't know where this Reema person gets off making these offensive assumptions about me—

IZZY

She'll be happy to hear it was a misunderstanding.

HOWIE

I mean, god, Izzy. And right after your shpiel about *us* not having faith in *you*. What do you *think* of me?

IZZY

I'm sorry, it's my sister. I had to ask.

HOWIE

Well you've asked.

IZZY

Indeed I have.

HOWIE

Jesus.

(Beat.)

I'll tell ya one thing, if I ever see this Reema *again*, I'm gonna tell her what I think of her talking shit about me.

IZZY

You should. She'll like that. *(Heads into the kitchen)* I'm gonna get some juice.

HOWIE

And for the record, I hope I *did* stiff her on the tip.

IZZY

Yeah well, for the record, you *did.*

(Left alone, Howie is reeling, but trying not to show it. He drinks his beer.

After a couple beats, Becca and Nat come in through the front door carrying bags of groceries. They're in the middle of an argument.)

NAT

Luckily she had read about it in the papers—

BECCA

Of course she did.

NAT

—so when I explained it, she realized who you were.

BECCA

You should've gotten her phone number. We could've had her over for cocktails.

HOWIE

Heyyy, they're back.

NAT

I was just trying to help.

BECCA

Well I don't need you chasing after me cleaning up my messes.

HOWIE

What happened?

BECCA

Or apologizing for me.

NAT

That's not what I was doing.

HOWIE

Did something happen?

IZZY

You get my message about the olive loaf?

BECCA

No, I shut my phone off.

NAT

I had to do *something*, Becca.

IZZY

(To Becca) Why?

BECCA

(To Izzy) Because you kept calling me.

IZZY

But I wanted olive loaf.

NAT

If I didn't say something, she would've had the cops there.

HOWIE

Cops where?

BECCA

She would not have called the cops.

NAT

You don't know that.

IZZY

Someone was gonna call the *cops*?

HOWIE

What *happened*?!

BECCA

Nothing.

NAT

We had a little scene, that's all.
(Regarding groceries) Lemme do this.

(Nat puts some of the groceries away. Becca moves to look over the sign-in sheet on the clipboard.)

BECCA

How'd we do here? Looks a little light, doesn't it?

HOWIE

What kind of scene? What *scene* did you have?

BECCA

In the supermarket.

IZZY

You and Mom?

NAT

(From the kitchen) No, I was not involved.

BECCA

It's so stupid.

HOWIE

What happened?

BECCA

This is why I hate shopping. Everything in there's like: "Oh look, Froot Loops, Danny liked Froot Loops. Hey, string cheese. Danny hated string cheese." Everything. Howie, you've got to do some of the food shopping. I'm sick of saying it.

NAT

(Comes back in) Becca got a little upset.

HOWIE

About what?

NAT

There was a boy there.

HOWIE

He reminded you of Danny?

BECCA

No. Maybe a little, but not really, no.

NAT

He had red hair.

BECCA

What happened was we were in the same aisle as this kid and he wanted these roll-ups, fruit roll-ups, and his mother was being a hard-ass about it, saying she wasn't gonna buy them for him.

NAT

And it wasn't because she couldn't afford it, because you could tell she had money.

BECCA

But the kid was getting whiny about it. Which makes sense, because he's five years old and he really wants these roll-ups, but the mother wouldn't give in. In fact she starts ignoring him completely, just turns her face away and pretends he's not there. Just goes about her shopping, like that's gonna shut him up, or teach him a lesson or something. Case closed sort of thing. But that only gets him *more* upset. So that pissed me off for some reason.

HOWIE

What did?

BECCA

The way she was ignoring him, instead of trying to explain why he couldn't have them.

NAT

So she walked over to her.

HOWIE

What? Why?

BECCA

I don't know. I just did.

IZZY

What'd you say?

BECCA

I said, "It's only three bucks, why don't you just get him the fucking roll-ups?"

HOWIE

Oh, no . . .

BECCA

And she looked a little miffed. But she smiled a little—I don't know why—and explained to me that she didn't want her son eating candy. And so I said it wasn't actually candy, in fact fruit roll-ups are relatively healthy, and they're made with real fruit, and why not give him a treat? And she told me to mind my own business, and then tried to move her cart around me, but ran over my foot by accident, so I smacked her.

(Beat.)

HOWIE

What?

BECCA

I smacked her.

NAT

She did. She smacked her. I couldn't believe it. Real hard too.

HOWIE

Becca . . .

BECCA

I know. It was awful, and then the boy started crying. I felt terrible, but she pissed me off.

IZZY

You hit that woman?

HOWIE

Izzy, don't.

IZZY

I'm just saying. Glass houses.

BECCA

She was *ignoring* him.

NAT

She *was* ignoring him. It was pretty bitchy.

BECCA

I wanted to shake her: "Look at him. Don't pretend he isn't there!" But I didn't say that. I just stood there, kinda startled, and she was kinda startled, and then Mom came over and told me to go out to the car, which I did not need her to do.

NAT

I just explained everything to her. That's all I did. And she was mad at first, but I explained it, and she understood.

BECCA

No she didn't.

NAT

After I talked with her, I'm saying.

BECCA

Still, she didn't understand, Mom. I'm sure you just made it seem like I was a crazy person. Some unstable—

NAT

You did slap her, Becca.

BECCA

She was lucky that was all I did!

(Nat shuts up about it, and goes back into the kitchen. Becca heads to the couch.)

Not that it *helped*. Not that she'll suddenly . . . realize . . . I mean, it was a *fruit roll-up*. Just let him *have* it. Am I wrong?

IZZY

No. I would've smacked her, too.

BECCA

Yeah, well, obviously.

(Beat.)

And I was doing well too, wasn't I, Howie? I had a bunch of good days in a row.

(Izzy snuggles up to her sister on the couch.)

IZZY

You can come shopping with me anytime, Bec. I'm gonna give my kid whatever he wants. Candy, whatever.

BECCA

That wasn't my point, Izzy.

IZZY

No, I know, you're saying *be* with him. She blocked him out instead of . . . appreciating him, or whatever. I understand. I totally get it. And if you ever see me doing what she did, smack me, too, okay?

(Beat.)

BECCA

Okay.

IZZY

Maybe you taught that lady something.

BECCA

Yeah, I don't think so.

IZZY

(Calls off) Hey, Mom, did they have any bosco?

NAT

(From the kitchen) Right here.

IZZY

Oh good, let's crack that bad boy open. *(Heads off)*

BECCA

(Off Howie's look) What?

HOWIE

Nothing.

BECCA

Have I shocked you?

HOWIE

No. Not shocked, no.

BECCA

Well you look shocked.

HOWIE

Do I?

BECCA

Or *something*.

(Taz starts barking. It immediately gets to Becca.)

Go quiet him down, wouldja, Howie?

(Howie turns to go. Jason is standing by the front door. He's entered, unnoticed. Pause. They all become aware of his presence. Nat and Izzy stand in the doorway of the kitchen.)

JASON

Hello. Hi . . . um . . . I saw the sign outside, so . . . the open house sign. And the door was open.

HOWIE

You looking to buy a house?

JASON

No.

BECCA

Howie—

HOWIE

What? He said he saw the sign.

JASON

I just wanted to say hey.

(Taz has not stopped barking.)

HOWIE

Taz! Shut up!

(Taz stops barking. They all stare at Jason.)

JASON

You know who I am, right?

HOWIE

Yeah, we know.

JASON

So, since the sign was out there, I thought it'd be okay if I just poked my head in. I've been wanting to say hello for a while and—

HOWIE

Now's not really a good time for us.

JASON

Oh. Okay.

HOWIE

We've got family visiting.

JASON

Right. I was just saying hey anyway. I didn't wanna bother you. Just say hello in person. But . . . maybe another time would be better.

HOWIE

Yeah. It's just we have relatives here.

JASON

Right, you said. Hi.

IZZY AND NAT

Hello.

JASON

Another time then.

BECCA

Yeah, we're . . . we're around, so—

HOWIE

Becca . . .

BECCA

What?

JASON

I could come by any afternoon really, if there's a day you're—

HOWIE

Well the problem is we're trying to sell the house, which takes up big blocks of our time.

JASON

It wouldn't take long. I just wanna sit down with you at some point.

HOWIE

Still—

JASON

I'd really like to arrange something if that's possible.

HOWIE

And I just told you now's not really a good time.

JASON

No, I know, but I wasn't talking about right now.

HOWIE

Great. So why don't you take off then? And if we can arrange something in the future we'll do that.

JASON

Okay. Well I wrote my number down . . . *(Pulls crumpled paper from his pocket)* So if you free up at all . . .

(More awkward silence. He places the number on the closest piece of furniture. He's about to go, when:)

HOWIE

Can I just say something to you? *(Advances on him)*

BECCA	NAT	IZZY
Howie, don't—	Hey, easy now.	Oh, Jesus.

HOWIE

An open house sign doesn't mean we're holding walking tours in here.

JASON

I know that.

HOWIE

You can't just pop in because the door's open. We were conducting business.

JASON

That's why I waited until that couple left. It looked like things were finished here.

HOWIE

Well they're not.

JASON

Then I apologize.

HOWIE

We *live* here, okay? This is our *home*.

BECCA

All right, Howie. *(Reaches for his arm)*

HOWIE

You don't just walk into someone's home like that. Especially given the *circumstances*. You should show a little respect.

JASON

I'm sorry. *(Looks to the others)* I'm sorry I interrupted.

(Beat.)

Sorry.

(Jason exits. They're all silent for a couple beats.)

HOWIE

You believe that? The balls on that kid? Walking in here?

NAT

(Regarding laundry soap) I'm gonna bring this . . .

(Nat heads into the laundry room with the soap.)

HOWIE

And what was he, out there hiding behind a tree or something? No wonder Taz was barking.

BECCA

Or maybe he was barking because he's hungry. Did you feed him?

HOWIE

Oh . . . no. I got caught up with—

BECCA

No, of course not. You wanted that dog so badly, but you can never remember to feed him. *(Turns to go)*

HOWIE

I'll do it.

BECCA

It's nice to know things are getting back to normal around here. *(Heads out back)*

HOWIE

(After Becca goes) That was the last thing she needed. That kid showing up.

IZZY

She seemed fine with it. You were the one who got upset.

HOWIE

Yeah, well, I'm not the one slapping people.

IZZY

(Regarding Jason) I don't know, you came pretty close just then.

(Pause.)

So I'm free next week if you wanna try this again. Another open house.

(Beat.)

HOWIE

Maybe. We'll see.

IZZY

You really should do something about that room though. Auggie does some renovation stuff on the side, if you want me to ask him. He could get in there and—

HOWIE

Oh, I don't know . . .

IZZY

He does good work. He put up my mother's drywall.

HOWIE

I think we got it covered.

IZZY

Still, you should really try to fix things up a little.

(Beat.)

The room, I mean.

HOWIE

Yeah, I know what you meant.

(Izzy heads into the kitchen, leaving Howie alone. The lights fade.)

Scene Two

About a week later. Nat is helping Becca clean out Danny's room. Becca is taking Danny's books out of a bookcase and placing them into a milk crate. Nat is taking toys, stuffed animals, kids puzzles, etc., out of a toy box and placing them into a garbage bag or keep box.

NAT

(Holds up toy) Keep or toss?

BECCA

Toss.

NAT

(Another) This too?

BECCA

Yeah.

(Nat puts both toys into the garbage bag. Becca finds The Runaway Bunny. *She flips through it.)*

Remember this one? *(Holds up the book)*

NAT

That was *your* book.

BECCA

I know.

(Becca puts it in the keep box. Nat pulls a Curious George doll out of the toy box.)

NAT

(Holds it up) Monkey?

BECCA

Um, keep, I guess.

(She does.)

NAT

Howie doesn't mind this?

BECCA

It was *his* idea. After that open house. Seems his grief goes out the window when it comes to maximizing profits.

(Beat.)

Sorry. I don't even know why I said that. Just being mean.

(They go back to work.)

Besides, it's not like we're getting rid of *everything*.

(Something stops Nat. She's holding a pair of Danny's sneakers. They're smaller than she remembers. Becca glances over at her and realizes what's happening.)

(Simply) Don't do that. *(Takes the sneakers)* Quick and clean, like a band-aid. *(Places the sneakers in a garbage bag)* Otherwise we'll never get through it.

(Becca grabs a kleenex from the bureau and passes it to Nat without missing a beat. She carries on as if the moment never happened.)

Did Izzy tell you I was taking a continuing ed. class? We're reading *Bleak House*. Isn't that hilarious? He handed out the syllabus and I just laughed. *Bleak House*. Of course no one knew what I was laughing at, which was *great*. *(Nat looks up at her)* It's in Bronxville so no one knows me. I'm normal there. That's what I like best about it. I don't get "the face" every time someone looks at me.

NAT

What face?

BECCA

You know. *(Demonstrates—solemn pity)* "Oh, hi. How ya doin'? Hangin' in there?"

(Nat laughs a little.)

I hate it.

(Together, they strip the robot sheets off the bed.)

And you know what's nice? These ladies, don't even *talk* about their kids or their husbands or any of it. I think they're just so happy to be away from all that. It's probably the *last* thing they wanna talk about. Because I'm sure most of them are bored housewives, right?

NAT

I don't know. I've never met these people.

BECCA

Well that's who takes Westchester continuing ed. classes, isn't it?

NAT

I guess.

BECCA

Sure, and they're just so happy to be talking about Dickens instead of what's for dinner. "Yay, we're reading literature." It's like they're in college again. Who'd *wanna* talk about their families? I know I don't.

(Beat.)

Anyway, I like it. I like that I'm just a lady taking a class. And next week we start *Madame Bovary*. That oughta get the ol' girls goin', huh?

NAT

I don't know that book.

BECCA

No, I know.

(Nat, packing up more toys, accidentally flips the switch to an obnoxious yapping dog. It's loud.)

NAT

What the hell? *(Trying to turn it off)* How do I—? *That's* annoying.

BECCA

(Over the noise) Try listening to it for hours on end! *(Switches it off)* Izzy gave him that. Only people without children give these kinds of gifts. Or people who want to punish parents.

(Then) You know what? Debbie's kids might like that. We should save it for *them*. That'd show her.

(Becca pops the toy into the keep box.)

NAT

Still haven't heard from her?

BECCA

Nope. Howie plays squash with Rick but . . . And I hear the kids are good. Do you remember Emily?

NAT

Of course.

BECCA

She's getting big now.

(Beat.)

NAT

I thought you haven't seen them?

BECCA

No, but . . . I passed by Danny's daycare last week, and the kids were all in the yard. *(Off her look)* What? I was just walking by. That's how I get to the post office.

NAT

Yeah. Anyway, that's too bad about Debbie. But that can happen. Friends disappear. I remember when Arthur died— *(Stops herself)* Sorry.

(Pause. Holds up a toy.)

What about this?

BECCA

No, it's busted. *(Takes it and tosses it)*

NAT

You know, the thing about Debbie . . .

BECCA

Yeah?

NAT

It's just as bad the other way sometimes. Do you remember Maureen Bailey?

BECCA

Sure.

NAT

Well I couldn't get rid of her after your brother passed away.

BECCA

I remember.

NAT

Always at the house. *Always* checking in on me. Eatin' up the cinnamon buns Uncle Jimmy brought me. I never had a moment to myself. And of course it was nice, I guess, but it didn't feel like it was about me. It just felt like she had nothing else to do. Like consoling me became her *hobby*. Something to fill up her day. And finally in the middle of coffee one afternoon, I said, "Maureen, why are you here all the time?"

BECCA

What'd she say?

NAT

She said, "I want to be there for you, Nat, I want to share in your grief." And so I said, "Well it's not working. I seem to have it all to myself still. You plant your fat ass in that chair every frickin' day—"

BECCA

You did not say that.

NAT

I did— "and suck up all my coffee, and I don't see you leaving with any of this grief you're allegedly *sharing* with me. In fact the only thing you *do* take outta here are my cinnamon buns."

(Beat.)

So I never saw her again obviously.

(Beat.)

Which was too bad actually, because she was the only one who was willing to talk about Arth— *(Stops herself again)*

BECCA

You can say his name.

NAT

Can I? I don't know your rules, Becca. I don't wanna get scolded.

BECCA

You can talk about Arthur. I just don't like the comparisons.

NAT

Okay.

BECCA

It's not like the Arthur stuff didn't . . . He was my brother, so obviously that was a really hard time for all of us.

NAT

I know.

BECCA

But that was a long time ago, and it was very different. For me.

NAT

Of course it was.

BECCA

Okay then.

(Back to work. Becca takes pictures off the wall. Nat finds some papers on a bookcase.)

NAT

What's this?

BECCA

Oh, it's a . . . It's just a story that boy wrote. He sent it to us.

NAT

(Regarding the title) What is it, an *Alice in Wonderland* kind of thing, or—

BECCA

No, it's more science fiction.

NAT

(Turns a page) It's dedicated to Danny.

BECCA

Yeah, he asked if he could do that.

NAT

Why? It's about Danny?

BECCA

No, not at all. It's about a scientist.

NAT

Oh.

BECCA

Or the son of a scientist, actually. The father discovers this warren of— It's like a network of holes to other galaxies, or parallel universes, I guess, but he dies somehow. And so the son goes into these holes trying to find him. Well not *him*, because he's dead, but another *version* of him.

NAT

It doesn't sound very good.

BECCA

It's okay. He's young.

NAT

Keep it?

BECCA

(Takes the story) Yeah, we should keep it. I'll just put it in the box.

(Becca puts the story inside the keep box. Nat goes back to cleaning. Becca contemplates telling her something, and finally relents. She tries to sound offhand.)

I think I'm gonna see him actually.

NAT

Who?

BECCA

Jason Willette.

(Beat.)

NAT

Why?

BECCA

I don't know. I just . . . want to.

NAT

What about Howie?

BECCA

Howie's not really into it.

NAT

Well I thought it was weird. The way he walked in like that. Creepy. You don't think that was creepy?

BECCA

Not really.

NAT

Well I think it was creepy. You should ask Howie what *he* thinks.

BECCA

I don't have to ask him what he thinks. Frankly I don't care what he thinks.

NAT

I'm just saying.

(After a beat, Howie appears in the doorway. He looks around. The bed has been stripped. The walls are bare. He regrets popping in, but it's too late now.)

BECCA

Hey.

HOWIE

How's it goin'?

BECCA

Fine.

HOWIE

Good.

(Beat.)

I thought we could put the brown bedspread in here.

BECCA

Okay.

HOWIE

And maybe hang the Ansel Adams prints that are in the basement?

BECCA

Sounds like a plan.

HOWIE

Making progress I see.

BECCA

Yup.

HOWIE

Good. Looks good.

(Pause.)

I'm gonna take Taz for a walk. You need anything while I'm out?

BECCA

I don't think so.

HOWIE

Okay.

(To Nat) Thanks for helping out, Nat.

NAT

Sure.

(He goes.)

BECCA

(Whispers) I hate that bedspread. I'm gonna put the blue one on. It's neutral enough.

(They work in silence. Nat suddenly smiles. She remembers something.)

NAT

Hey, you know what I was thinking of this morning?

BECCA

What?

NAT

(Chuckling a little already) Remember that gourmet basket you and Howie got me for Mother's Day last year, with the biscotti and the fancy biscuits? And I put the chocolates out when you came over for dinner, and Danny ate the entire bowl of chocolates when no one was looking?

BECCA

(She's heard this story many times) Yup.

NAT

And then Howie was like, "Where'd all the chocolates go?" And I said, "Danny ate them. Leave him alone, kids like candy." And then Howie said, "But those were chocolate-covered espresso beans!" Remember?

BECCA

I do.

NAT

But Danny had eaten the whole bowl, so he was, you know, really really wired. And running in circles and climbing up the walls, and putting things on his head, and he was up until like three A.M. Remember that?

BECCA

Only too well.

NAT

I didn't know what the damn things were. I just thought they were candy. You get me these fancy baskets with all this crazy stuff in 'em—espresso beans. I tell that story to everyone. People get a kick out of it.

(Becca smiles.)

BECCA

(After a beat) Mom?

(Nat looks up at her.)

Does it go away?

NAT

What.

BECCA

This feeling. Does it ever go away?

(Beat.)

NAT

No. I don't think it does. Not for me it hasn't. And that's goin' on eleven years.

(Beat.)

It changes though.

BECCA

How?

NAT

I don't know. The weight of it, I guess. At some point it becomes bearable. It turns into something you can crawl out from under.

And carry around—like a brick in your pocket. And you forget it every once in a while, but then you reach in for whatever reason and there it is: "Oh right. *That.*" Which can be awful. But not all the time. Sometimes it's kinda . . . Not that you *like* it exactly, but it's what you have instead of your son, so you don't wanna let go of it either. So you carry it around. And it doesn't go away, which is . . .

BECCA

What.

NAT

Fine . . . actually.

(They're silent for a couple beats. Becca nods a little. She goes back to work. So does Nat.

The lights fade.)

Scene Three

A few days later. Jason is sitting on the couch in the living room. He looks around. Becca enters from the kitchen with a plate.

BECCA

I made some lemon squares.

(She holds out the lemon squares, and he takes one and a napkin.)

JASON

Thank you.

BECCA

Can I get you milk or something? I don't have any soda. Unless you want seltzer.

JASON

I'm fine.

BECCA

You'll need something to wash it down though. You don't drink coffee, do you?

JASON

Sometimes.

BECCA

You want coffee?

JASON

No thanks. Really, I'm okay.

BECCA

All right. But let me know if you change your mind.

(She joins him on the couch. Jason takes a bite of lemon square.)

JASON

It's good.

BECCA

Thank you.

JASON

Still warm.

(She smiles. Pause.)

So, you're moving?

BECCA

We're thinking about it. If we can find a buyer.

JASON

Where are you moving to?

BECCA

We're still looking.

JASON

Far away?

BECCA

Probably not, no. My husband works in the city, so we can't go that far.

JASON

What does he do?

BECCA

He works at Prime Brokerage. Risk management.

JASON

(Doesn't know what that is) Uh-huh.

BECCA

He takes the train in.

JASON

Right.

BECCA

So we don't wanna go too far.

JASON

It's a nice house. I hope you find one as nice as this.

BECCA

We'll probably go smaller. This is too big.

(Jason goes back to the lemon square.)

I'm sorry Howie couldn't be here.

JASON

That's okay.

BECCA

He's, uh . . .

JASON

Not ready?

BECCA

I was gonna say working, but yeah, *that* too.

JASON

He seemed mad. The other day.

BECCA

No, he was just surprised that you dropped by.

JASON

Okay.

BECCA

You just scared him a little bit.

JASON

He didn't seem scared.

BECCA

Yeah well . . . Maybe that's not the right word. But . . . Howie's not mad at you. What happened was an accident. Howie knows that.

(Beat.)

You know that, too, right?

(Jason takes a bite of lemon square. Taz barks out back. Becca cringes.)

That bark goes right through me. I swear, we better move somewhere without squirrels.

JASON

You should have his vocal cords snipped.

BECCA

What?

JASON

That's what some people do. If their dogs won't stop barking.

BECCA

Huh. I've never heard of that.

JASON

Yeah, because some dogs just never shut up. So that's what they have to do. Otherwise the alternative is give 'em away. Or put 'em to sleep, I guess. You should look it up online. I bet there's all sorts of information, if you're interested.

BECCA

No, Howie would never allow it. He loves that dog too much.

(Beat.)

Do you have any pets?

JASON

No.

BECCA

Well that's lucky.

JASON

Yeah?

BECCA

Unless you *want* a pet. Do you want a pet? Because I've got one you can borrow. Just kidding.

(Pause. Jason notices a book on the coffee table.)

JASON

We read that book.

BECCA

Bleak House?

JASON

Yeah, in English class.

BECCA

Did you like it?

JASON

Not really. It's too long.

BECCA

I know. I barely made it through.

JASON

I liked *David Copperfield* though.

BECCA

Also very long.

JASON

Yeah, but it didn't feel as long.

BECCA

No, you're right.

(Pause.)

JASON

So, I don't see any photos anywhere.

BECCA

Of Danny?

JASON

Yeah.

BECCA

Well, we put most of them away. Because of the open house.

JASON

Okay.

BECCA

Do you *want* to see pictures? Because I could—

JASON

No thank you.

(Beat.)

BECCA

Okay.

JASON

The one in the article was nice though. Him at the beach.

BECCA

That's at Anneport Bay.

JASON

I used to have a shirt just like that one. The one he's wearing in the picture.

(Beat.)

I might've been going too fast. That day. I'm not sure, but I might've been. So . . . that's one of the things I wanted to tell you.

(Beat.)

It's a thirty zone. And I might've been going thirty-three. Or thirty-two. I would usually look down, to check, and if I was a little over, then I'd slow down obviously. But I don't remember checking on your block, so it's possible I was going a little too fast. And then the dog came out, really quick, and so I swerved a little to avoid him, not knowing, obviously . . .

(Beat.)

So that's something I thought you should know. I might've been going a little over the limit. I can't be positive either way though.

(Pause.)

BECCA

I'm gonna get you some milk. You don't have to drink it if you don't want it.

JASON

Okay.

(Becca heads into the kitchen. She gets a glass from a cabinet and fills it with milk.)

BECCA

So you're a senior?

JASON

Yeah.

BECCA

Where you headed in the fall?

JASON

Connecticut College. They have a good writing program.

BECCA

Oh, well that's nice for you. And not too far from home. Your parents must be happy about that.

JASON

It's just my mom, but yeah, she's happy about it. She's already started picking out sheet sets for the dorm room.

BECCA

Uh-huh.

JASON

She keeps saying she's gonna apply to the graduate program so she can keep an eye on me while I'm up there. She's just joking though.

BECCA

Right.

JASON

She's not really looking forward to it, since I'm the only one at home now, but I told her I'd come back on the weekends when I could.

BECCA

That'll be nice.

(She reenters, brings him the milk.)

There ya go.

JASON

Thanks.

(He puts the milk down.)

BECCA

And you graduate when?

JASON

Thursday. Matt Lauer is gonna speak. His niece is in my class.

BECCA

Well that's great. I like Matt Lauer.

JASON

Yeah. So does my mom.

BECCA

So you must have a prom coming up then.

JASON

It was last Saturday actually.

BECCA

And you went?

JASON

Yeah.

BECCA

Do you have a girlfriend or—

JASON

No. I mean, I *did*, but we broke up a while ago, so I went with this girl Carly who's just a friend, and this other girl Tina went with this guy Jake whose dad owns this old-fashioned Rolls-Royce that he brings to car shows and stuff, so we all went in that together.

BECCA

That must've been fun.

JASON

Yeah, it was a tight squeeze though, because no one wanted to sit up front, but it worked out. We had champagne in the back—not to get drunk or anything, just to celebrate—but Carly is really skinny so she got a little tipsy, even though she barely had like one glass of champagne. And she kept telling the driver to put the top down because she wanted to stand up in the back and act crazy, but the car wasn't even a convertible, so we essentially made fun of her all night for that. That part was pretty funny.

(Becca has been tearing up while listening. And with little warning, she is crying. A lot. It goes on for a few beats. Jason just sits, not sure what to do.)

BECCA

I'm sorry.

JASON

No, that was stupid of me.

BECCA

I asked.

JASON

Still, I shouldn't have— Should I go?

BECCA

No. I'm fine.

(She collects herself. She grabs a kleenex and blows her nose.)

I'm sorry.

(They sit in silence for a couple beats.)

So did you have a good time? At the prom?

JASON

It was okay.

BECCA

Well it sounds like it was very nice.

(Beat.)

I liked that story you sent by the way. I'm sorry we never thanked you for it.

JASON

That's okay.

BECCA

We appreciated it.

(She grabs another kleenex and wipes her nose.)

So the scientist that the boy is looking for . . .

JASON

Yeah?

BECCA

Is that your dad?

(Beat.)

JASON

No.

BECCA

I mean, is it based on him?

JASON

No. My dad was an English teacher.

BECCA

Oh. Okay. I was just curious about that part. He is dead though, right?

JASON

It's just a story.

BECCA

No, I know. I'm sorry. It's none of my business. I was just . . .

JASON

Reading into it?

BECCA

Yeah.

(Beat.)

Well, anyway, I liked it very much. It reminded me of Orpheus and Eurydice. Do you know that Greek myth?

JASON

Not really.

BECCA

Eurydice dies, and Orpheus misses her so much, that he travels to Hades to retrieve her, but in the end it doesn't work out.

JASON

I should read it.

BECCA

Yeah, it's similar. But instead of Hades, you have the rabbit holes. The parallel universes. It's interesting. I liked that part.

JASON

Thank you.

BECCA

Is that something you believe in?

JASON

Parallel universes?

BECCA

Yeah.

JASON

Sure. I mean, if space is infinite, which is what most scientists think, then yeah, there *have* to be parallel universes.

BECCA

There *have* to be?

JASON

Yeah, because infinite space means . . . it means it goes on and on forever, so there's a never-ending stream of possibilities.

BECCA

Okay.

JASON

So even the most unlikely events have to take place *somewhere*, including other universes with versions of us leading different lives, or maybe the same lives with a couple things changed.

BECCA

And you think that's plausible.

JASON

Not just plausible—probable. If you accept the most basic laws of science.

BECCA

Huh.

(Beat.)

So somewhere out there, there's a version of me—what?—making pancakes?

JASON

Sure.

BECCA

Or at a water park.

JASON

Wherever, yeah. Both. If space is infinite. Then there are tons of you's out there, and tons of me's.

BECCA

And so this is just the sad version of us.

(Beat.)

JASON

I guess.

BECCA

But there are other versions where everything goes our way.

JASON

Right.

(Beat. A change.)

BECCA

And those other versions *exist*. They're not hypothetical, they're actual, *real* people.

JASON

Yeah, assuming you believe in science.

BECCA

Well that's a nice thought. That somewhere out there I'm having a good time.

JASON

(After a pause) So, could you tell your husband for me? How I might've been going a little over the limit? I know he's probably still mad but—

BECCA

He's not mad. Nobody's mad.

JASON

Okay.

(Beat.)

Can you tell him though?

(Beat.)

BECCA

Sure.

(Jason goes for the milk. He drinks it as the lights fade.)

Scene Four

Eat-in kitchen. Dusk. Nat enters with a box of toys and books from Danny's room. She places them on the table. Izzy follows, reading The Runaway Bunny.

IZZY

I don't remember *The Runaway Bunny* book being so weird. The mother's like a stalker.

NAT

Oh come on. She's not a stalker.

IZZY

Well of course *you* don't think so. But look, she turns into wind and shit, a mountain climber. Poor kid needs to get himself a restraining order.

(Izzy puts the book in the box, and finds the obnoxious yappy dog toy she had given to Danny.)

Heyyy, I remember this. She said I could have it?

NAT

Oh yes, that one *especially* she wants you to have.

(Becca enters with a recipe she's printed out for Izzy.)

BECCA

Here. I typed it all out for you. I put down lime zest in the filling, but you can also use orange zest, or even a little grapefruit. Or lemon, obviously.

IZZY

(Looking at the recipe) Jesus. It's like three pages long. This looks hard, Becca.

BECCA

It's not. I promise. I put everything down.

IZZY

I hope the oven works. I don't think Auggie's ever used it. He keeps dishes in there.

BECCA

If you get stuck, you can call me.

IZZY

Okay.

(Beat. Chuckles.)

Me—baking. Auggie's gonna be shocked.

NAT

Well, anyone in their right mind *would* be.

IZZY

Ha ha.

(Howie enters, home from work, calling as he enters:)

HOWIE

Hello-hellooo . . .

(He's carrying something in tinfoil. Becca is surprised to see him.)

IZZY

Hey, Howie.

NAT

Hello.

HOWIE

Hi.

BECCA

You're home.

HOWIE

(Taking off his jacket) Yeah.

BECCA

I thought you had group.

HOWIE

I decided to skip it.

(Beat.)

IZZY

Mom, we should get going, if you wanna get to bingo.

NAT

Why, what time is it?

IZZY

We gotta *go*. Auggie wants me to register for lamaze, so I can learn how to shove a baby out of my body.

(Regarding box of toys) Thanks for the stuff.

BECCA

You're welcome.

IZZY

Bye, Howie.

NAT

(To Becca) Bye, sweetie.

HOWIE

Bye, guys.

(As they exit with the box of stuff . . .)

NAT

Bingo's just at Saint Catherine's, you know. What's the bum's rush for?

IZZY

Can we talk about this in the car please?

NAT

I didn't even get a lemon square.

(And they're gone.)

HOWIE

(Regarding tinfoil) Alan brought in his zucchini bread again. He made me take what was left. He wants you to try it.

BECCA

That was nice of him. You'll have to thank him for me.

(Howie gets himself a beer.)

We had paillard if you're hungry. It's in there.

HOWIE

No, Alan kept pushing that bread on me all day.

BECCA

Okay.

HOWIE

(After a couple beats) So how'd it go with the kid?

BECCA

Fine. It was totally fine.

HOWIE

What'd he want?

BECCA

Just to . . . I don't know, introduce himself, I guess, talk a little.

HOWIE

Did you let him off the hook?

BECCA

What do you mean?

HOWIE

Well, he seemed pretty intent on sitting down with us. I assumed he wanted to be absolved or something.

(No response.)

Is that what he wanted?

BECCA

Not really. Not in so many words, no.

HOWIE

Huh. Did you tell him we didn't blame him?

BECCA

We *don't* blame him.

HOWIE

No, I know, but did you let him know that?

BECCA

I guess so.

(Beat.)

HOWIE

That's good.

(Beat.)

So I don't have to meet him then, do I?

BECCA

Not if you don't want to, no.

HOWIE

Okay.

(He sits at the table.)

BECCA

Why aren't you at group?

HOWIE

I just decided to skip it tonight. Wasn't up to it.

BECCA

How come?

HOWIE

I think I might be done. With the group. I don't think I'm gonna go back.

BECCA

Why, what happened?

HOWIE

Nothing. I just don't think it's as helpful to me anymore. I wanna try it on my own for a while. I mean, not on my own, obviously, but . . . without the group.

(Beat.)

That sound okay?

BECCA

Sure. If you're not getting anything out of it then why go?

HOWIE

Exactly.

(Beat.)

BECCA

Are you okay?

HOWIE

Yeah. I'm just tired. And full of zucchini bread.

BECCA

All right. I'm gonna have a piece. It's good?

HOWIE

Yeah, it's great.

(Becca goes to cut a piece of the zucchini bread.)

BECCA

So Rick and Debbie invited us over for a cookout this weekend.

(Beat.)

HOWIE

Really?

BECCA

Sunday they said. Are you free?

HOWIE

Yeah. You talked to Rick?

BECCA

No. Debbie.

HOWIE

You talked to Debbie.

BECCA

Yeah. I called her.

HOWIE

Wow. She must've been surprised.

BECCA

She was.

HOWIE

What'd she say?

BECCA

Oh you know, she cried mostly, and then apologized about sixty times, and then cried some more.

HOWIE

Sounds great.

BECCA

It was okay. She said she kept meaning to call, but she felt freaked-out about everything and so she kept putting it off, and before she knew it months had gone by, and so then she *really* couldn't call because she felt like such an asshole, and assumed I hated her, so it just seemed easier to not pick up the phone.

HOWIE

And that was good enough for you?

BECCA

I don't know. Probably. We'll see how the barbecue goes.

(She joins him at the table.)

HOWIE

Are the kids gonna be there?

BECCA

Of course.

(Beat.)

HOWIE

That'll be hard.

BECCA

Yeah. It'll be good to see them though. We should get something for Emily. We missed her birthday. She turned four last week.

HOWIE

Right. Okay.

(Beat.)

Danny's is coming up.

BECCA

I know.

HOWIE

That's gonna be a tough one.

BECCA

Yeah.

(Silence as Becca eats the bread.)

(Regarding zucchini bread) It's good.

HOWIE

I'll tell Alan you liked it.

(More silence.)

It's so quiet.

BECCA

That's because I slipped Taz a couple Ambien.

HOWIE

(Smiles) You're funny.

BECCA

You think I'm joking.

(Becca takes another bite of zucchini bread.)

(After a beat) You think we should reconsider the house?

(Beat.)

HOWIE

If nobody bids, we might have to.

BECCA

There are worse things, I guess.

HOWIE

Yeah.

BECCA

It's a nice house.

HOWIE

I know.

BECCA

(After a pause) So what are we gonna do?

HOWIE

About what?

BECCA

I don't know, pick something.

HOWIE

Well . . . *(Thinks it over)* We could go to Village Toys tomorrow and pick up Candy Land for Emily. That's probably something she'd like.

BECCA

Okay, Candy Land. That's a start. Then what?

HOWIE

Then we wrap it.

BECCA

Uh-huh.

HOWIE

And then on Sunday we go to the cookout, and we give her the gift, and we talk to Rick and Debbie, and to make them feel comfortable we ask the kids a bunch of questions about what they've been up to, and we'll pretend that we're really interested. And then we'll wait for Rick and/or Debbie to bring up Danny while the kids are playing in the rec room. And maybe that'll go on for a little while. And after that we'll come home.

(Beat.)

BECCA

And then what?

(Beat.)

HOWIE

I don't know. Something though. We'll figure it out.

BECCA

Will we?

HOWIE

I think so. I think we will.

(Silence. They just sit for several beats, not even looking at each other. They're scared.

Then Becca takes Howie's hand. They hold on tight.

And the lights slowly fade.)

END OF PLAY

Author's Note

Rabbit Hole is a delicate play tonally, and its balance can be easily thrown out of whack. With that in mind, a little guidance from the playwright . . .

Yes, *Rabbit Hole* is a play about a bereaved family, but that does not mean they go through the day glazed-over, on the verge of tears, morose or inconsolable. That would be a torturous and very uninteresting play to sit through. The characters are, instead, highly functional, unsentimental, spirited and, often, funny people who are trying to maneuver their way through their grief and around each other as best they can. Sure, they hit bumps along the way, and are overcome by various emotions, but I've tried to be very clear about exactly when and how that happens.

It's a sad play. Don't make it any sadder than it needs to be. Avoid sentimentality and histrionics at all costs. If you don't, the play will flatten out and come across as a bad movie-of-the-week.

Tears: if the stage directions don't mention tears, please resist adding them. Howie gets some at the end of Act One. Becca cries at one point during her scene with Jason. Nat might *almost* cry when she finds Danny's shoes in his room. But I think that's about it. I'm pretty sure Izzy doesn't need to cry in this play. And I *know* Jason shouldn't cry, ever. (Yes, he's haunted by the death of Danny, but his emotions aren't especially accessible to him. Please, no choked-up kids openly racked with guilt. That's not who he is. Restraint, please.)

Laughter: there are, I hope, many funny parts in the play. They are important. Especially to the audience. Without the laughs, the play becomes pretty much unbearable. Don't ignore the jokes. They are your friends.

Please, no extra embracing, or holding of hands. Avoid resolution at all costs. Becca and Nat, for example, shouldn't hug at the end of their scene in Danny's room. It's not that kind of play. There can and should be moments of hope and genuine connection between these characters, but I don't ever want a moment (not even the very end) where the audience sighs and says, "Oh good, they're gonna be okay now." *Rabbit Hole* is not a tidy play. Resist smoothing out its edges.

DAVID LINDSAY-ABAIRE is the author of *Fuddy Meers*, *Kimberly Akimbo* (L.A. Drama Critics Circle Award, Kesselring Prize, Garland Award), *A Devil Inside*, *Wonder of the World* and *Rabbit Hole*. His plays have been produced at theaters throughout the U.S. and around the world, including Manhattan Theatre Club, Minetta Lane Theatre, Soho Rep, Woolly Mammoth Theatre Company, South Coast Repertory and the Arts Theatre on London's West End, among others. David is currently working on the Broadway-bound musicals *High Fidelity* and *Shrek*. He is a graduate of Sarah Lawrence College and the Juilliard School, as well as a proud member of New Dramatists, The Dramatists Guild and the Writers Guild of America. He was born in Boston, and currently resides in Brooklyn with his wife, Chris, and their five-year-old son, Nicholas.